MISTER FAKE DATE

AN ESCORT ROMANCE

MIKA LANE

Join Mika's Insider Group
www.mikalane.com
Contact Mika

Copyright© 2019 by Mika Lane
Headlands Publishing
4200 Park Blvd. #244
Oakland, CA 94602

ISBN ebook 978-1-948369-20-6
ISBN print 978-1-948369-21-3

CHAPTER 1

CLOVER

There are few things more pathetic than a guy who thinks he's *all that*, but is *so not*.

And at that moment in time, I was confronted by this very essence of douche-baggery—a pain-in-the-ass dude trying to make himself look more impressive than he was.

"Clover," Nat said, gazing around the sumptuous country club party I'd been forced to attend. He seemed to believe he could successfully get into my pants while scanning the crowd for someone more interesting to talk to.

Seriously. The dude thought he could wear me down without even making the effort to look me in the eye? I'm not a demanding chick, not by any stretch of the imagination, but at the same time I do demand some R-E-S-P-E-C-T.

Did men like this actually get laid?

"You look great tonight," he continued in a surprised tone, as if I usually looked like shit. His eyes continued to scan the room when someone bumped his arm. His Moscow Mule splashed all down the front his ill-fitting shirt where buttons strained over his belly, and an ice cube clattered to the floor.

"Thank you," I mumbled. A Brazilian bikini wax would be more fun than I was having at that moment.

His full name was Nathaniel Jessup. To his face I called him Nat, but behind his back, my sister and I called him *The Jester*. His fake smile was nearly as annoying as his fake laugh.

No, I was not a fan of the one man in the world my mom was convinced was my soul mate. It was testament to how little she knew me—that she'd pressure me to be with such a douchebag.

"Your mom tells me you need a date to your sister's wedding." Clearly proud my mom had confided in him, he hitched up his trousers, exposing his hairy, sockless ankles.

Thanks, Mom.

"Well, that was nice of her. But I'm good. Really."

"Yeah, well I thought maybe I could help you out, and that we could go together."

Did he not hear what I just said?

"Thanks, Nat, but I don't need a date."

"But you're going, and I'm going, so why don't we go together?" He winked at me—why, I was not entirely sure. Maybe this whole thing was a conspiracy between he and my mom? Forces joined to ruin my life?

"No, that's okay. I appreciate your asking, though." Now *I* scanned the room. Where was my sister when I needed her most?

Either he wasn't listening, or he had something wrong with his hearing. "We'll probably be sitting at the same table anyway—it makes sense that we go as dates. You know what I mean?" he asked like he was making me the offer of a lifetime.

I did know what he meant. But there wasn't enough money in the fucking universe to get me to be The Jester's date.

"Really, Nat, I'm good."

If I could have wiped the condescension off his face without disgracing my family, I would have. "Clove"— where did he get off giving me a nickname?—"everyone knows women hate going to weddings dateless. Let me help you out. You know, so you don't look like the family's old maid."

He did *not* just say that.

I leaned toward him and smiled as sweetly as possible, but there was acid in my voice, the kind people in certain social circles use, where words flow like honey but sting so fast you're not sure what happened.

"Nat. I said no. Thank you."

He shook his head and smiled. "All right, Clove. When you are ready to swallow your pride, just let me know. I'll be here. No judgment."

I stood stiffly when he gave me a one-armed hug, and watched him wander off to the buffet table, where he'd been scarfing shrimp all night. I had half a mind to tell him to lay off them. They were doing nothing for his horrendous breath.

But fuck him. I didn't owe anyone who called me an *old maid* a damn thing.

Not only was The Jester a douche, but he was also a dork. At the caliber of party we were attending—a birthday party for my father's best friend and oldest business associate—*no one* ever ate. It's not that there wasn't a ton of food. No, on the contrary, you could have fed a small village with the spread offered at this and every other party just like it. It's just that no one wanted to look as common as needing food. The women were rail thin and fought like hell to stay that way, and the men just drank most of their calories. And heaven forbid someone photographed you with food in your mouth, or worse, chewing. That would bring on shame of one of the highest degrees.

No, the food, plentiful as it was, would all be trashed at the end of the night. Or sneaked home in the backpack of some resourceful waiter.

"Sweetie, I saw Nathaniel and you chatting," my mom said as she approached me in an ivory silk pantsuit, looking like a million bucks.

Which was funny, because she had way more than a million bucks.

"Yes, Mom, we had a little chat," I said, taking a deep breath for control.

She scanned the crowd, looking for him. "He sure looks handsome tonight." I marveled at her invisible pores. She was always perfect, never had a hair out of place. She could even eat without messing up her lipstick.

But one area she might have needed looking into was getting glasses. If she thought The Jester was even remotely attractive, she surely she needed them.

"Mmmm-hmmm." I was inches from using one of my 'escape' excuses. I had an arsenal of them, ranging from the basic *I have cramps*, to the more desperate *my roommate just called and thinks our place is on fire*.

Mom put a hand on her hip. "I don't know why you play so hard to get with him. He's a wonderful young man, and I know he cares about you."

If she weren't so blinded by ambition and her obsession with her daughters making good marriage matches, she might have seen the real Nat. But my mother seldom saw the real anything—only what she wanted. And the fact was, The Jester's family had something she valued. Prestige and money. The perfect storm.

"Mom," I said, glancing at my watch, "I have to head back to L.A. I have class in the morning."

She looked at me sympathetically, like I was off to do something dreadful along the lines getting a cavity filled.

"Darling. You really don't have to do that." Her face was beatific. I don't know how she did it.

Botox, maybe?

"Do what, Mom?"

I knew what she was talking about, but I wanted her to say it.

She sniffed impatiently. "You know. Go back to that horrible apartment. And job."

Okayyy. There we had it, out in the open. *Honey, you don't need to work, much less study for your master's degree. Silly girl.*

"Uh-huh. Thanks, Mom. I'll be heading out now." I set down my wine glass and slung my purse over my shoulder.

But she grabbed my hand, pressing a small wad of cash into it, like she often did. "Sweetie. You could always move home, like Jessamyn, and fill your days like she does."

Fill her days? All she did was plan her wedding. And shop. And I happened to know she was bored as shit. There were only so many ways to spend money before you got into the absolutely stupid, and Jess wasn't that vapid.

"I know I could do that, Mom. But I want to do something with my life other than charity luncheons and shopping excursions."

She made a small, high-pitched laugh. She didn't say it, but I knew she was wondering how she got such an alien for a daughter. Sometimes, I wondered the same thing. If we hadn't looked so much alike, I might have had my DNA tested.

When I'd finally escaped, I got to my Prius and kicked off my red-soled Louboutins, happily replacing them with my black high-top Chucks. The Loubs went into the trunk, under a pile of blankets and towels I kept in my trunk for impromptu beach days.

There were some parts of my life I kept to myself.

"Hey, I'm home," I yelled, walking into the apartment my mother had decided was 'quirky.' She really thought it looked like a crack house, I'd overheard her telling my sister.

Who says stuff like that?

"Yo," my roommate, Sarah, said, coming into the kitchen where I was putting on tea. She was little and perky, and was going to make the perfect teacher with her passion and love of all things kids. "How was the birthday party?"

This was where the 'keeping things to myself' part came in. Sarah was sweet, but the Loubs in my trunk cost more than her share of the rent.

"It was all right. Kind of boring. You know, a bunch of old people."

What I didn't tell her was that people had arrived in limos, that there'd been a U.S. senator and two members of Congress in attendance, or that there wasn't one woman's handbag in the crowd that cost less than ten thousand dollars.

No, when you wanted to fit in with the other broke graduate students getting their master's degrees in elementary education, you didn't share that your dad built private jets sold all over the world, or that your family home was an estate in the hills above Santa Barbara overlooking the stunning California coast.

You kept those things to yourself, like the Louboutins

in the trunk, hidden under beach blankets and a slew of lies—like that my purse wasn't actually a knockoff I bought from a street vendor in downtown L.A., but the actual, designer real deal.

"What did you do tonight?" I asked.

"Well, let's see. I finished my lesson plans for the week, then went to the taco truck down the street. So good, and so cheap. Hey, speaking of cheap, Macy's is having a huge sale, if you want to go tomorrow." Her face lit up at the word 'sale.'

"Yeah, sure," I said, thinking of the five one-hundred-dollar bills my mother had pressed into my hand on my way out of the party. She'd tasked me with finding a nice dress for my sister's rehearsal dinner, which meant Neiman Marcus or Saks. Not Macy's.

I'd never even been in a Macy's until one of my college roommates had taken me there. 'Course, I hadn't let on. I acted like I shopped there all the time. I'd found a few things on the sales rack and was initiated. It was actually fun to find a couple bargains.

I grabbed my tea and headed for my room in our graduate student apartment. "I have to get a lesson ready for tomorrow, too. I'll be leading an art class."

"Oh, that sounds like fun. Way more fun than the reading lesson I need to lead."

I wasn't sure how much fun it was going to be, trying to teach a roomful of seven-year-old kids how to paint with watercolors.

But it would sure be a lot more fun than the party I'd just come from.

"Joshua, please don't put paint in Caitlyn's hair."

It might have been smarter to just stick with crayons and coloring. But no, I had to get creative. Teach the little ones something new.

And now there was paint all over the damn classroom.

I'd studied business as an undergraduate. Thought I'd go to work for my dad's company and build private jets for the richest people in the world. But after a couple summer jobs working in the mailroom and as a general office gopher, I realized the business world was just never going to float my boat. I needed something where I was interacting with lots of people. Something where I didn't sit on my ass all day and plug away at a keyboard while stressing over numbers and dealing with investors.

"Miss Clover, tell him to stop," wailed another little one whose name I was always forgetting.

I couldn't let my supervisor know I didn't have all the kids' names down pat. They placed a big premium on that sort of thing. Mandy, Mindy…maybe Myndy with a y and an accent. I could never quite be sure.

So I crouched down next to her instead. "Sweetie, who's bothering you?"

She pointed to a dough-faced little turd with a smug look on his face sitting just next to her.

I knew that look. It was exactly what The Jester wore when he made me the offer of a lifetime. Cripes, did it really start this early, with the creepiness and the inability to understand the word *no*?

"Did you hear her say *stop*?" I asked him.

With a confidence I didn't know was possible among seven-year-olds, he shrugged like he'd done nothing wrong. "She likes it. I know she does." And he rolled his eyes and turned back to his painting.

Holy shit.

I'd had it. I knew what I needed to do to help out my little girlfriend who was being harassed, and I knew what I had to do to help myself.

"May I have your paintbrush, young man?"

He turned to look at me like I was bothering him. "Fine," he said. Then, to my surprise, he slapped the paint-covered end of the brush right into the palm of my open hand, leaving me looking like a jar of mustard had exploded there.

My bad for not anticipating that as a possibility.

"Okay, buddy," I said, grabbing his hand with my paint-covered one, "you're coming with me."

He shrieked when he realized he, too, now had bright yellow paint all over his hand. But I held his little paw firmly in my own and marched him down to the principal's office where I hoped he'd learn a thing or two about respect. I left him sitting in a chair way too big for a kid, sniveling about the mess in his hand.

The rest of the art lesson came off without a hitch, and

to be honest, I was quite pleased with my class of mini Picassos and Matisses.

On the drive home from school, I knew it was time to do something for myself. I dialed my best friend, Hen.

"Henrietta Rousseau here," answered an efficient voice.

I knew how much she hated her name, and it always shocked me when she actually said it out loud.

"Yo. Hen. It's me," I said, picturing her long red ringlets. We'd been friends since elementary school, sticking together even through undergrad. I'd not seen her in ages and needed to remedy that.

"Oh, hey. I thought you were my new pain-in-the-ass client."

A snicker escaped me. "You mean your new pain-in-the-ass client who's going to be paying you shitloads of money, right?" Her public relations firm had fairly exploded in the last eighteen months. Of course, it didn't hurt that one of her first clients was my dad's company.

"Yeah, yeah," she replied with a snort. "So what's up?"

"Hey, so you know how my sister's getting married, right?" I asked.

In the background, I heard her close her office door. The firm she ran was loaded with gossipy bitches.

"Of course, I got the engraved invitation myself. Kidding. I know I'm not invited. But when it is, anyway? And is she still marrying that douchebag Robert?"

"Soon. And yes. Man of her dreams, and all that."

"Gag," Hen said, laughing. She went through men faster than anyone I'd ever seen.

I sighed. "I know, right. But hey, I need a date for the shindig, and The Jester is all over me. I gotta show up with someone. You know that place you told me about?" I asked. "Where you get your itch scratched?" Those words made my skin crawl, but they got right to the point.

"What place?" she asked, then *ooooh'ed* happily. "Yeeeessss, Player. Welcome to the dark side, my beotch. You gotta call them! Their guys are a-mazing."

"Yeah, well, what I need is a date, not *that*," I replied, although I could have used *that*, as well. "Text me their number? I'll call today to line something up. It feels weird as hell, but it would be worse to show up dateless and be subject to The Jester's harassment. I'm already the black sheep because I want to teach, and now even more so that I didn't manage to get married before my younger sister."

On the other end of the line, I heard the door to her office open. She muttered, "Thank you," most likely to some harried intern. "Shut the door!" she screamed after the poor soul before returning to her inside voice. "It's weird at first, being out with one of those guys. But you'll find they're just nice, normal men. Well, normal in public."

You never knew what Hen meant by 'normal.'

"Cripes, how many men have you gone out with through the place?"

"Just a couple. One when I needed someone for a business dinner, and another when I was just horny as hell. You wouldn't believe what I did with that guy," she said, humming. "He was so huge I could hardly—"

"*Stop.* I don't want to know. Just send me the info." She

loved nothing more than sharing the details of her, um, *rendezvous*.

"Only if you promise to tell me everything," she said. "I mean pinky swear, got me?"

"Hen, there won't be anything to tell. He's just gonna be my date for my sister's wedding."

Yeah, right.

CHAPTER 2

WILL

I brushed the wrinkles out of my trousers as I got out of my car. It was barely nine a.m. when I arrived at Player —my new employer. The sun was shining, and the day was already bright. I rang the bell, still wondering how I'd ended up working here. The door buzzed, and I opened it to see a seriously buff guy in the lobby, looking like he just walked out of a Calvin Klein underwear commercial.

I extended my hand. "Hi... I'm Will. I'm the new guy."

"Hey, I'm Xander. Welcome aboard." This was the dude I was supposedly replacing. "Let me show you around a bit," he said, leading me down some stairs to a private gym.

And what a gym it was. It was nearly empty, save Xander and me and a very fetching attendant folding towels in the corner. The place was outfitted with state-of-the-art weights and cardio equipment, a steaming hot tub in one corner, and in the other, a wooden door that read *sauna*. Through big glass doors, I could see a lap pool outside with a few lounges scattered about, and a massage table under a white awning.

I did a three-sixty to take it all in. "Is this all for us?"

"Yeah. Sweet, isn't it? Just for the guys who work here." Xander looked wistful. "Zenia really takes care of us. I'm gonna miss all this," he said, nodding.

"You got a role in a movie, right?"

It wasn't hard to believe. The guy had serious movie-star looks and was built like a damn fighter.

"I did get a role, yes. But I also have a steady partner now. I didn't feel right about continuing in the biz when I wanted to commit to someone."

"I hear ya." I'd wondered how the guys handled that sort of thing. But it was too soon to ask, and I didn't have anyone serious anyway.

"Let's head outside to run a couple miles. Then, we'll come back and do weights. Seems crazy to do cardio indoors on such a gorgeous day," he said.

"Lead the way."

I let Xander set the pace, and damn if he wasn't fast. I mean, I was in good shape, thanks to my swimming scholarship at UCLA, but this guy ran like a gazelle.

"What's your story, Will? You got a girl?" he asked, not winded in the least.

I followed him around the corner to a quieter street where we were able to get off the concrete sidewalk and run on the softer asphalt pavement. "No, no girl for me.

My plate's kind of full at the moment. I'm working to get custody of my kid sister since our parents passed, and it's proving to be harder than I thought it would be."

"Oh man, sorry to hear about your parents."

I wiped a bead of sweat from my brow. I was sorry this guy was leaving Player—it was always great to run with someone in such good shape.

We stopped at a red light, and I worked to catch my breath. "Thanks. So between losing our parents, finishing school, and trying to keep my sister out of trouble, things are kind of crazy."

"Damn, you aren't kidding," Xander said.

"So what's it like?" I asked.

"What's what like?"

"You know, escorting. Taking women on dates. For money." I could hardly believe I was saying the words out loud. I'd been haunted by images of taking advantage of lonely old ladies and hoped to god I was wrong. There was no way I could do that. Ever.

"It's actually awesome," he said, brightly. The light turned green and he took off with me a half step behind. "You hang out with these lovely ladies—they're all beautiful in their own way, you'll see—and you don't have to do anything you don't want to. If you do meet someone you're attracted to and want to get down and dirty—well, if she's into it—it's all good. But that's considered 'off the clock.'"

"What does that mean, 'off the clock'?" I asked.

"Oh, right. I guess Zenia didn't have time to explain much to you. 'Off the clock' means it's not part of the agreement between Player and client. In other words, it takes place separate from any arrangement, and is technically outside the agreed-upon appointment time."

"Sounds kind of contrived to me."

"It's a strange formality, but it keeps Player on the right side of the law—something Zenia is *very* big on."

"Okay. I get it. So we pretend we don't sleep with clients, but we actually do," I said.

"We do sleep with clients, you are right, but not always. In fact, it happens less often than you might think. You wouldn't believe how many women I accompany to the ballet or opera, or just take to a party or dinner. Or, I guess I should say *used to*," he said with a laugh. "I am going to miss some of those good seats at the opera. It's actually fun, once you figure out what the hell's going on."

Regardless, the arrangements Xander described didn't sound half-bad, which was a relief—I'd be lying if I didn't admit I'd come into things with a shit-ton of trepidation. But I needed some steady income—it had to be *good* income—and I needed it right away. The food truck gig I'd had with my buddies was just not going to cut it since I'd taken on responsibility for my sister.

It was crazy how, in a second, life could change so much. One day you're going to college on a UCLA swim team scholarship, living the good life—the next, your parents are T-boned by a truck and killed. And you are the one and only person who can take care of your sixteen-year old sister because your only other living relatives have dementia. I'd always thought most things in life changed slowly, over time, like how the oak tree in my parents' front yard became twenty feet tall, or my dad's hair turned salt-and-pepper gray. But boy, was I wrong. Seemed the most impactful things happen in the blink of an eye. So I guess the key was not to blink.

Yeah, right.

We'd gotten back to the brick building that served as headquarters to Player, and we headed in for part two of our workout.

"So, have you seen many clients, yet, Will?"

"Not yet. I think Zenia is starting me out slow," I replied, recalling her 'training' the last two weeks. She was quite the, um, instructor...

Xander increased the weight on the bench press after I'd finished my set. Christ, I was a wimp next to him. "She just...approved me."

"Yeah, she does that. Lets you come up to speed slowly," he said.

"Well, the second client I had was more steamy than the first. I'm not really sure about this work, honestly. It feels a little weird."

"Don't worry. Everyone feels weird at first. It's natural. And it's not for everyone. If you aren't digging it, there's no shame in that."

"Thanks for saying that, man. I appreciate it," I said.

"Sure thing. I might not be with Player any longer, but you can call me anytime you want to talk."

~

Xander had split not long after we'd done weights, something about having to get back to the studio. It sounded like he had little or no free time anymore, so I was doubly honored he'd made time to hang out with me and tell me about the biz.

The lap pool was freaking amazing, and possibly for the first time since losing my parents, I got into a groove, slicing through the water, lap after lap. I've always loved the water for that. My mind calmed until it was occupied with peaceful white noise, and before I knew it, nearly an hour had passed and I'd swum two miles and then some.

That's what I'd always loved about swimming. The rhythm you got into where you didn't have to think about what you were doing. You just did it, and an amazing meditative state followed. It was like crack for me, really.

And I had access to this amazing pool that was tiled in blue and green to make it look like the Caribbean Sea. I had a feeling I'd have it to myself most times.

That was what I called a *bonus*.

I showered and dressed and took a moment to rough my hair up with a thick, white towel. Ready to face the world again, I headed out, only to run smack into my new boss, Zenia.

"Will. I was hoping I'd catch you down here," she said with a megawatt smile.

Christ, she was gorgeous in her floaty beige pants and top—the perfect contrast to her lush brown skin and amber-like eyes.

"Oh, hey, Zenia. I didn't think I'd run into you. I've

heard you're usually sequestered in the penthouse upstairs."

She let her head fall back as she released a throaty laugh. "I know. That's what everyone says. 'We never see you, Zenia. We just get your text messages.' Like *Charlie's Angels* or something. But hey, if you have a few minutes, can you come upstairs for a chat?"

"Sure thing." I racked my brain over what I might have done. Could I have screwed something up already? Or was she...wanting more training?

I'd never been in a penthouse before, but let me just say, it was something I could seriously get used to. Zenia's office was like something out of freaking *Architectural Digest*, only warmer and more lived-in. Everything was soothing, from the white walls to the leather furniture. The elegance suited her perfectly.

"Take a seat, Will," she said, gesturing to the chairs opposite her desk. "Would you like some tea?"

"No, thank you."

She folded her hands on the desk where she sat. "So I want to welcome you again, even though you've been with us a couple weeks. I hope your time with Xander went well and that he was able to share some useful information."

"Great guy. Thank you for setting that up. I'm looking forward to seeing his movie."

"I am, too. It's all very exciting." She flipped open a slim folder on her desk and shuffled a couple papers until she found what she'd been looking for. She looked back up at me. "I have a client that I think you might be a good match for."

My heart started to beat a bit faster. Maybe this gig wasn't for me...I mean, I liked to get laid as much as the next guy, but getting paid for it? It just felt *weird*.

I guess there were worse ways to make a buck.

"I have a new client who needs a boyfriend. It's kind of a special engagement, and it's for several days. You would be staying on-site with the client at a family gathering."

She stopped and looked at me, as if she were waiting. I guessed that was my cue to ask questions.

So I did. "All right. Why did you choose me, might I ask, over the other more experienced guys?"

"Good question, Will. I chose you for a few reasons. One, you're close in age to this woman. But also, you're an athlete, and an outstanding student. And last, is that by sending you—a relative unknown—there is little to no chance of anyone recognizing you as being from Player. The...social class of the gathering means the chances of an Agency client being in attendance are greater than your average Los Angeles gathering."

Good thinking.

I continued. "What about physical contact?"

Surprise crossed her face. "You didn't seem to have a problem in training—are you uncomfortable with the idea? It's certainly not required, but I wouldn't want to put you in a position of doing something you'd rather not."

"No, I'm not saying I'm objecting to anything. I just want to go into things with my eyes wide open."

"Well, you will be sharing a room with this woman, as part of the charade. If that doesn't work for you, I have a couple other guys I could check with. But if it helps at all, the pay is twenty-five thousand dollars."

Um, what?

I leaned closer to her in case I'd misheard something. "How much?" I asked.

She smiled. I was sure she knew very well that the number would seal the deal. "Twenty-five thousand dollars. It's good money, Will. Very good. And all off the books."

No shit.

"Can I let you know first thing tomorrow morning?" I asked.

She sighed and scribbled something on a clean notepad.

Of course her notepads were clean.

"Yes, but please let me know as early as possible. It's very important that this client is well-taken care of."

"I'll call first thing." I headed for the door. "And Zenia?"

She looked up at me. "Yes, Will?"

"Thank you for the opportunity. I'm honored."

She just smiled as I pulled the penthouse door closed behind me and headed for the elevator.

I wished I'd asked her one more time—had she really said *twenty-five grand*?

I headed to my parents' house in the Valley, where I'd

moved back to after they'd passed, in order to stay with my sister. The meeting I'd had with a family court judge just the day before replayed itself in my head.

"Mr. Adams, you are petitioning for custody of your younger sister, Charlene Adams?" The black-robed older woman had a kind, maternal look about her. But she spoke in a no-nonsense clip. God knew what sort of shit she'd seen over the years in a family court.

Chili cringed. She hated being called Charlene.

"I am, Your Honor."

Out of the corner of my eye, I saw my sister doing her rotten teenage thing. I'd coached her until I was blue in the face that if she didn't behave appropriately in court, who knew if she'd get to stay with me or not. But in spite of my advice, she stood in her typical slouch, with her arms folded tight across her chest.

I got it, I really did. Losing our parents had been awful. Shit, it *still* was awful. But it had hit her especially hard. She was just a kid—how was she supposed to process her parents dying in a car wreck on their way home from a run to the grocery store? All our lives had changed in an instant. The worst of it was that she'd been the one to answer the door when the cops came with the bad news.

How fucked-up was that?

Her turn came to speak to the judge.

"Miss Adams—may I call you Charlene?" the judge asked.

"Actually it's Chili. Call me Chili," she said, smiling. At least she was pretending to be cheery.

"Chili," the judge said, flipping through some papers. "Is Chili your given name?"

She nodded. "Yes, it's my given name. I gave it to myself."

Amused, the judge made a few more scribbles on her pad. "Do you want to live with your brother, Chili?" he asked.

She shrugged. "I guess so."

Jesus, sound a little more enthusiastic.

"Either you do, or you don't, Chili." The judge's tone was still clipped, but clear. "This is court, not high school. I cannot deal in unclear answers where I have to guess your meaning."

"Sorry. I do. I do want to live with my brother. Where else would I live?" she asked.

"We could put you in the foster system, but it's always our preference for families to remain together."

Chili glanced at me nervously. I'd told her foster care was a possibility. But she hadn't believed me until that moment. "Please, I want to stay with my brother."

The judge turned to me. "Mr. Adams, I do have some concerns that you need to finish your college degree and have no way to support yourself and your sister since your scholarship ended. I see your parents didn't really have an estate to leave behind."

I wasn't sure whether the judge was patronizing me or not, but I sure as hell chafed against her assumptions.

"Judge, I just need some time to get together a plan. I can support us and finish my degree next semester," I said.

A kindly old lady like that wouldn't split up a brother and sister.

Would she?

"I'll tell you what. Child Protective Services is beyond overwhelmed right now," she said, pointing at the papers before her. "And according to what you've submitted to the court, you are at least temporarily able to support yourselves. Let's pick this up again in thirty days and see where we are."

I breathed a sigh of relief. I couldn't let anyone take Chili. If there was one thing I knew my parents would have wanted, it would have been for me to look after my sister. That left me with only one choice, I realized as I steered my Jeep into our parents' driveway.

I had a very important call to make to Zenia.

CHAPTER 3

CLOVER

It was probably just as well I was in my work clothes. And glasses.

I wasn't sure how much Player guy who I was supposed to meet knew about me, but I might as well look like a total frump because he was going to think I was a big loser, anyway. I mean, how pathetic was it I was hiring a guy to take me to my sister's wedding?

Yeah, I could have just shut up and gone with The Jester. But I knew better than to force myself to try and stomach an entire weekend with him. If I couldn't tolerate him for five minutes last week, how the hell would I make it through several days of his smarmy ass?

Even the thought of it made me crave a shower to wash it off.

"Hi, are you Clover?" a deep voice said from before me.

Shit. I'd been so lost in thought I'd stopped watching the coffee shop's front door. I'd wanted to see my date before he saw me, in case he looked like bad news.

But he did not look like bad news, just like Hen said he wouldn't. On the contrary. Christ, when Hen said Player had a stable of thoroughbreds, she had not been exaggerating.

My new friend, should he care to accept my mission, was probably one of the—if not *the*—most handsome men I'd ever laid eyes on. Thick black hair, a little on the messy side, like he finger-combed only and it looked *good* like that, dark eyes with disgustingly lush eyelashes (why did guys always get the good lashes?), and a dimple on one cheek.

Not only that, but his slightly faded polo shirt was snug across a very nicely defined chest and set of shoulders, and his waist narrowed above some slim khaki trousers that showed off a well-honed physique. I guess I wouldn't have expected any less, but that didn't take away from the marvel that was the man before me. The gods were on their best behavior the day they'd invented him.

"Hi…hi. Yes, I'm Clover." I stood to shake his hand and smashed my knee on the edge of the table. "Aw…shit!"

"Watch it there. You okay?" he asked, grabbing my arm to steady me.

No, I wasn't okay. My knee hurt like hell…but the touch of his hand on my arm made me forget my problems, if only for a minute.

But I smiled. "Oh, yeah, I'm fine. Just being a klutz. Had a long day. You must be Will."

"I am." He stood there expectantly while I sank back into my seat and rubbed my wounded knee.

Then it dawned on me. I needed to invite him to sit. Christ, I was a dolt.

"Please, have a seat, Will," I said, pushing my glasses up on my nose and gesturing to the chair opposite.

"I like your specs," he said, his gaze glued to mine. "Funky nerdy. Very cool."

"Oh. Right. Thank you. Yeah, I usually wear contacts." I pulled them off and tucked them into my purse. The room became a bit blurry, but I could still see the man across from me just fine.

"You're so pretty, Clover."

Wow. He didn't waste any time.

"Ha, you probably say that to all the girls." I snorted.

His head snapped back, and his mouth opened to speak. But then it closed just as quickly, and he pushed his chair back to stand.

Oh no. I'd offended him, and now he was leaving. Didn't anyone have a sense of humor anymore?

"I'm getting coffee. Can I get you something?" he offered.

Oh. He wasn't leaving. Good.

"No, I'm good. I'll just wait here." I gave him a weak smile, and spilled a drop of my latte thanks to a trembling hand.

Okay, so far so good. My big mouth hadn't driven him

off yet. And why should it, anyway? I mean, I wasn't asking this guy to freaking marry me. Just spend a few days with me, for which he'd be handsomely paid. I'd think he'd have thick enough skin to put up with my verbal diarrhea.

Before I knew it, he was heading back to the table, which meant I could no longer stare at his ass. If all went according to plan, there'd be time for that later.

"So, Clover," Will said, sitting back down, "tell me about the upcoming festivities."

Oh boy. Where to begin? "Well, my mom is all over me to date this family friend whom I cannot stand. He's the biggest ass. So I figured if I showed up at my sister's wedding weekend with my own date, they'd leave me the hell alone."

"Makes sense to me." He rested his elbows on our little table, and looked around the coffee shop. "I guess we've all got that one person we'd rather die than date."

Damn if something about him wasn't a little rough around the edges. Not that he was rude or anything—it was just that he was so...normal. Not the fancy type that usually moved in my circles. Or my family's circles, actually.

Perhaps I should have called Player and asked for someone different, maybe a bit more refined, but I actually liked that this guy wasn't overly polished. Give me a guy who was too perfect and I fell right into a snoozefest. It was the ones who'd been around the block, and had some stories to tell about it, that really were my kryptonite.

"So what's your story? What do you do with your day?" he asked.

He looked at me like he suspected I laid around all day eating bonbons, but knew better than to actually say it. I knew how people like him judged people like me. It was why I kept my real background under wraps when I was with 'normal folks.'

"My story?" I asked. "I'm earning my graduate degree in elementary education."

His eyebrows rose. It seemed we were both doing a bit of judging the other, and for some reason I found myself hoping I'd just scored points with him.

"No kidding. My mother was an elementary school teacher," he said, suddenly looking down at his coffee and nodding. "And my dad was a high school teacher."

"Really? Where do they teach? If they're in the L.A. school district, I might know them."

He sat back in his chair and looked at his coffee. "No, they taught out in the Valley. And they're not teaching anymore, anyway. They recently passed away."

Whoa. *Both* parents?

"Oh my god, I'm so sorry. Geez. That must be rough," I said, the words all tumbling out.

"It is." He looked up at me with a small smile.

"How long have you been ah…escorting?" I blurted out.

I could ask that, right? Or was such a question against etiquette? Damn, why hadn't I thought to ask Hen that before I put my big foot in my big mouth?

31

"I haven't been doing this long. I think that's part of the reason we were matched up."

"Really? You didn't tell Zenia you wanted some poor girl who couldn't get a date to her own sister's wedding?" I laughed a bit too loudly.

But he didn't laugh at all.

Instead, he reached for my hand. "There's nothing to be embarrassed about. Nothing wrong with wanting someone to take you to an event."

His hand felt good. Warm, and safe, with fingers that just about devoured mine.

Time for some practicalities. I pulled my hand back and put it in my lap. "Okay. Since you're new and all, do you think you can be doting, but not overly so? You know, so we look like a real couple? Just want to get us on the same page if we're going to do this."

What did I mean 'if we're going to do this'? Of course we were.

"I don't know that 'doting' is really my style," he said, simply.

Oh. Snap.

"Um, would you excuse me while I run to the ladies'?" I asked. I needed to call Hen.

And don't you know, when I was just a few feet away, I overheard him mumbling, "What the fuck am I gonna do for five days...?"

I turned back to see him, arms tightly crossed, looking out the window. Cripes. He was a prickly one. But I kind of liked that. Actually, I really liked that.

I pulled out my phone and speed-dialed my friend, who answered on the first ring.

"Hen? Do you have a sec?" I asked.

I heard her shut her office door. "Yeah. Aren't you supposed to be meeting with your guy from Player?"

"I am right this moment. I excused myself for the ladies' room," I said.

"Oh, I gotcha. I'll bet he's gorgeous. All the guys there are."

"He is, for sure. Look, I have to ask you a question. He seems a little…I don't know…difficult."

"Really?" she asked. "That sounds kind of hot. But if you don't like it, let Zenia know. It's up to you, and her customer service is G-spot-on." She laughed at her cheesy joke.

"Okay. I just wanted to check and see if you could, you know—trade them in for another model."

"Oh my god, girl, you are so bad. Look, I gotta go. I see three interns pacing outside my door. Little punks…"

"Okay. Thanks," I said, and swiped my phone closed.

Will watched me walk back to the table, making me wish I'd worn something a touch more appealing. But I liked the way he appreciated me while I crossed the room.

"I think we're all set," I said, not sitting down.

He stood. "All right, sounds good. Hey, wait. How did we meet?"

Yes. The details. Where the devil lurked. "Oh right. Um, at a party at my neighbors.' How's that sound?" I asked. "I guess we should swap some more details—nothing too elaborate, though, right?"

He smiled and that damn dimple returned. "Sounds good to me. Let me walk you to your car."

When we got to my Prius, I decided to test him a bit. It was a beautiful L.A. night, and the palm trees made me feel a smidgeon romantic. "You know, Will. Before you go, I was thinking you might kiss me good night. Just for practice."

Without missing a beat, he inched toward me, tilting his head like a damn sex god. "Really? Is that really what you think?" he asked, pulling a frown.

Shit. Maybe I should have kept my damn mouth shut. "Um well, you don't have to…"

But before I could let him off the hook, I realized he was playing with me. He slowly ran his fingers over my cheeks. One of his hands reached through my hair and—

"Oh!"

He'd grabbed a fistful and pulled. Hard, but not too hard.

Oh my god, oh my god, oh my god. He was the bossy type, and I was in trouble, now. I was going to be spending five days with this man? Even if he were a bit of a roughneck?

Truth be told, I absolutely could not wait.

"Told you, I'm not the doting kind," he said right before his lips closed the final fraction of an inch.

∼

"Jess, it's me," I said when my sister picked up my call.

"Hey. What's up?" It sounded like she was driving. Probably in that Porsche SUV her douchebag fiancé had bought her. He'd only done it to impress my parents. It was so obvious, at least to me. But how did he think getting a Porsche would impress a man who made jets like my father's?

I took a deep breath. "Hey, I'd like to bring my new, um, guy to your wedding."

The background noise went quiet. Had she actually pulled over to the side of the road? "You have a new guy? Since when?" she asked. Fair question, to be honest.

I told the first of a slew of lies. "Well, uh, I've known him only a short time…"

A really short time…

"…but long enough to know he's great. You know, I like him and I thought it might be nice to, um, bring him. To your wedding. As a date."

"Of course it's okay. But Mom thought you'd go with Nathaniel."

My darling sister had no idea how badly she'd just insulted me.

"The Jester? Ugh, even saying that name makes the bile rise in my throat. I have someone else to bring, Jess. Someone I've been *dating*." I needed to practice saying that out loud.

Dating. The loathsome D-word.

"Sure, of course that's fine. Who's the guy?" she asked. The background noise started up again, and I assumed she was driving, her initial shock at my having an actual date having dissipated.

"Will. Will Adams."

"Do I know him? Does the family know him?" she asked.

Shit, I hoped not.

"I don't think so. We met in the student apartments on campus. At a party."

"Oh, a student. Like you. That's nice," she said. She would probably be the only person all week who'd say that.

Cripes, I needed to really have my story straight. My sister's questions were no doubt just the tip of the iceberg. Other family and friends would *really* put me through the third degree. Especially my mother.

And even more important was making sure Will's story was in synch with mine. All we needed to do was start telling different people different accounts, and we'd have the fun of facing a disaster of epic proportions. On those *Lifetime* channel romances I watched it was cute. But probably not in real life.

Things were already getting more complicated than I'd anticipated. Perhaps I could just call it all off. Skip the whole wedding. I did have a painful ingrown toenail I could use as an excuse.

Nah, I couldn't bail on my sister's wedding.

"Yeah. He's great. I'm looking forward to your meeting him. He's very nice-looking."

That was an understatement. Wait till she saw him. She'd have a freaking heart attack. In fact, she probably wouldn't believe a guy like that would ever date a girl like me. Shit, even *I* knew a guy like that would never date someone like me.

But as long as I was able to stay away from The Jester, I wouldn't worry about what anyone else thought.

Next call was Hen.

"Okay. It's all set up," I said, reporting back.

"Ohhhh, my girl's taking a walk on the wild side, isn't she?" she cooed. "I can see you now. You got your glasses and student teacher clogs and cropped pants on, and one of those blouses with the shoulders cut out—what do they call those? *Cold shoulder* or something? And he comes along all hot as shit. Like the school marm and the prince."

Was I *that* bad? Spending her days at a fancy P.R. firm wearing designer clothes out the ying-yang, she had no idea what it was like to try to blend in with a school full of soccer moms. "Glad to know you think I'm such a dud."

She laughed. "You know I'm kidding. You're hot…when you want to be."

Was that a compliment? Or an insult?

"Hey, does he know about the Lufkin fortune?" she asked, conspiratorially.

"I've filled him in on some stuff, for cover story. If he doesn't believe me, he will the moment he sees the estate. But what worries me a little is being discovered. You know, by family and stuff."

Well, I had more than a little worry about all that.

Hen snorted. "Oh my god. You have nothing to worry about. You know how often these sorts of arrangements happen? All. The. Time. It's very common and accepted."

"If it's so accepted, why do people keep it on the down-low?"

"Oh. Well, I don't know. But there's no shame in it. Hey, when you're done with your guy, do you think I should try him out?"

Seriously?

"That's gross, Hen. Let me finish with him first. Then you can do whatever the hell you want."

I pictured her propping her four-inch spike high heels up on her desk. Mistress of the universe. "When do you see him next?"

"When he arrives at my parents' place for the festivities."

"Send me pics. I want lots of pics," she demanded.

"Yeah, yeah. Of course there'll be lots of pics. It *is* a freaking wedding."

CHAPTER 4

WILL

After letting Zenia know I was on board with the Lufkin job, I had to give notice at the food truck where I worked with my buddies. A bunch of guys in my business class had started it as a weekend gig, and I'd helped with the operations, occasionally serving the fried chicken they were becoming so famous for. Sometimes I even got paid. It had been a shoestring operation, and every last penny was pinched until it squeaked. It had been great business experience for us all, and I knew if anything else, I would be able to take a good fried chicken recipe away from it.

But when my parents passed, the money for school had to be used to keep a roof over Chili's and my head. UCLA might be able to give football and basketball players scholarship money galore, but a swimmer like me who wasn't an

Olympic hopeful? Scholarships don't cover everything. Tough luck, sorry for your loss, and we'll wish you all the best in your future endeavors. And don't even think about qualifying for a student loan, since you don't have anyone to cosign for you.

It was brutal.

That's when I realized I needed a job where I made *real* money—actually, more than real money—I needed a shit ton of money to prove to the court I could take care of my sister. A start-up food business where the biggest perk was going home Saturday night with a six-piece box of chicken was simply not going to cut it.

"Dude, this is your last day with us?" my buddy Devin asked, as we tried not to trip over each other in the cramped space. Who knew the inside of a decommissioned old mail truck was so small?

I'd filled up a Styrofoam box with fried chicken for Chili's and my dinner and wiped greasy fingers on my apron as I took it off for the last time.

"Yup. I'm sorry I can't stay with you guys and see where the business goes. I'm really bummed about that. But duty calls."

Devin nodded, and paused as he counted out the cash box for his shift. "Hey, I get it. We all do. You need to make some real money now, while I'm still doing this more for the class credit than anything else. You've got big responsibilities. You'll be a great bodyguard. Just be careful." He clapped me on the back, shook my hand, and I was off.

Yes, *bodyguard*. It was the first of many lies I'd be telling in the coming weeks.

I'd told Chili the same. I mean, I wasn't about to tell my kid sister about Player or all that that entailed. Instead, my cover story was that I was a bodyguard—nothing too dangerous—but I was required to do a bit of travel. I just had my fingers crossed she'd be okay on her own for a few days.

I was headed back home to help her with homework and to pack my things for Player gig, when my cell rang. The call was coming from an unfamiliar number. I'd usually let such a call go to voicemail, but something told me to answer it.

"Mr. Adams? Is this Mr. Adams?" a bureaucratic voice asked over a staticky line.

Shit, was I overdue on another bill? I'd been fighting off bill collectors for weeks. "Yes, this is Will Adams."

"Mr. Adams, my name's Sergeant Akins from the Los Angeles County Sheriff's department."

Huh?

"What can I do for you?" I asked, my pulse picking up.

"Mr. Adams, do you have a sister, Charlene Adams? Sixteen years old?" he asked.

Okay. What the fuck was going on?

"Yes, what happened? Did something happen to her? Tell me what's going on."

Papers shuffled in the background while the officer continued. "She's fine, Mr. Adams. Your sister is fine. She's just gotten herself in some trouble."

It was only four o'clock in the afternoon. She was

supposed to be home doing schoolwork.

What the hell?

"Seems she and some friends 'borrowed' a car and took a little joyride. They crashed it into a row of shopping carts at the grocery store. They tried to run away, but security caught them."

Jesus. Fucking. Christ.

I was going to kill that kid. Well, not really, but she was going to be put on restriction, for sure.

Or something like that.

I'd never put anyone on restriction. I wasn't even sure how to do it.

"Can I come get her? Do we need bail or anything?"

"No, it's a minor citation at this point that won't require bail, but I can only release her to a guardian. She told me your parents were deceased?"

"Yes, Sergeant, I am her guardian since our parents... um...passed," I lied. Hopefully by the time they figured out I was not her guardian, I'd have her home. Where she'd be on restriction. Big-time.

"Okay then, Mr. Adams, you can come get her. She will have to appear in juvenile court, but you'll be informed of when that is via mail."

"I'm on my way."

When Chili was permitted to pass through a locked door into the beige, cinder-block waiting room where I sat with a bunch of other pissed-off parents, she ran to me, all gangly arms and legs. The second my arms were around her, she started to sob.

"I'm sorry, Will, I'm sorry. I won't do it again."

I rubbed my hand over her long hair like I'd seen our mom do. "C'mon. Let's get out of here."

She hung on me on the way to the Jeep. "One of my friends told me they were allowed to borrow the car," she said on the drive home. "Then, when we were already driving along, he said he actually didn't have permission to use it, but that he wanted to teach his bitchy neighbor a lesson. At first I thought it was all fun and stuff, but then he crashed." She sniffled and looked out the window. "God it was all so stupid."

"Chili, you can't be doing stuff like this."

I glanced over at her, and she just nodded.

Time for some tough love. "Do you want to go to a foster family? Have to pack up all your stuff, go live with strangers, and most likely have to attend a new school?"

She shook her head violently. "No, Will, please don't make me do that."

I reached across the seat and wrapped my hand around her fingers. "It's not up to me. Seriously. If you can't get your act together, the courts will take you away from me. That'd kill us both, which is why I'm trying so hard to get custody. But I need your help, Chil. We could be split up if we don't get it together."

"I'm sorry," she said quietly, nodding. "I...I'll do my best, I promise."

"Well," I say with a small smile, "you don't have to be anything but Chili inside the house. I love my little sis, not some robot girl."

"That's good," Chili says with a laugh. "All the robot girls I know about end up having the guy fall in love with them. Ew, that would be waaaaay too awkward."

I pulled up to our house, but we didn't get out of the car.

I turned to my sister. "Remember, I have a job that I need to travel to and will be gone five days. Can you keep your nose down for that long?" I asked. "Just Friday through Tuesday, maybe Wednesday morning?"

She nodded furiously. "Yes, I will. I swear, no drama."

"Okay. You remember my friends you met from my new job, Sandy and Richard?" I asked, remembering two of the other guys I met during my 'basic training' with Player. They swore to keep my secret from Chili, and they seemed trustworthy. "They'll check in with you, and Mrs. Jones from next door will, too."

"Okay."

"I'm sorry I have to leave you, especially now, but this is a chance for me to make a big chunk of money for us, which will help in our case for my becoming your guardian."

"Okay. I'll be fine." She looked down at her hands, nodding.

"Remember, when you pull stuff like this, you're not letting me down. You're really letting down Mom and Dad," I said with a lump in my throat.

I hated to play the deceased parents card, but if there was ever time to do it, it was then.

"I miss them so much," Chili said, bursting into fresh tears.

I leaned across the front seat and pulled her into my arms. "I miss them, too. Believe me, I miss them, too."

Mrs. Jones, our angelic neighbor, had, as a fellow teacher, known my parents pretty well. She'd agreed to keep an eye out for Chili while I was gone, and even promised Chili would eat better than leftover fried chicken and delivery pizza every night. While I left town with more than a shit-load of trepidation, I knew I had to do the Lufkin job, and do it well.

The ride up the coast from L.A. to Santa Barbara was stunning, especially with the top down on my Jeep, and served to clear my head a bit. I bounced along in the fresh air with classic Neil Young playing full volume. He'd been my dad's favorite, and while it wasn't totally my taste, it was a reminder of what I needed to do, and why.

I followed the GPS to the address Clover had given me, and when I got closer, things started to make sense. I'd wondered how the hell a schoolteacher, dressed pretty much like a nerdy librarian—but a very pretty one—could spend twenty-five grand on a date for a wedding.

And when I saw the house—or should I say *compound*—she'd invited me to, everything made sense.

After climbing a steep and winding road into the hills of Santa Barbara, the elevation testing the horsepower of my old Jeep, the road opened to something that looked like a freaking palace. Huge Spanish arches, lots of adobe-style walls, and palm trees...everywhere along the driveway there were palm trees. I could even smell oranges in the air, and I wondered if I would have the chance to find them during my visit. It wasn't picking season, but that didn't change the wonderful smell.

I pulled into a circular drive and looked back at the direction I'd just come from, amazed again by what I saw. I had a clear view of the Pacific Ocean, glistening in the morning sun. Behind the house, mountains rose up—or I guess officially they were hills. Honestly, it didn't matter. It was still dramatic and breathtaking.

"May I help you, sir?" A deep voice yanked me out of my trance.

A strangely formal man in khakis and a polo shirt stood ramrod straight at the bottom of the stone steps leading up to the front door, a slightly officious look on his face. Was he some sort of butler or something?

"I'm Will Adams."

He looked at me blankly. I was either at the wrong address, or no one had told him I was coming. I still had time to leave, but the thought of twenty-five grand floated over my head like a rain cloud.

The good kind of rain cloud.

I stood on my seat and jumped out over the car door to exit the Jeep. It was the best part of having a convertible, although it was easy to see butler-guy was taken aback by my Tarzan-like move. "I'm, um, Clover's friend," I said, reaching into the back seat for my hanging bag and duffel.

Butler boy nodded and gestured while offering to take my bag. "Ah. Miss Clover. We were expecting you. I'll show you to her cottage."

Cottage? Did he just say freaking *cottage*? Like, she didn't stay in the Big House?

Christ. What had Zenia gotten me into?

What had I gotten *myself* into? And why had my parents gotten into a fatal car accident, leaving me and Chili to figure shit out alone?

I looked up at what looked was a toss between sprawling mansion and fancy hotel. Seriously, it looked like the sort of spread Hollywood execs would have, or LA business leaders, or maybe even some A-list movie star.

"Do you...work here?" I asked, extending my hand.

Shit. What if he were Clover's dad?

"Yes, Mr. Adams. I am one of the staff." He shook my hand anyway. "Please, call me Sanders."

And I was now an official douche.

Zenia had hinted I needed to be prepared for this gig. She'd loaned me Player credit card, sent me to a tailor for my suits and tux, and then sent me off to what I guessed was a very expensive hairdresser. Personally, I didn't think my hair looked much different when I was finished, but hey, who doesn't love a shampoo and head massage?

I looked up to see Clover running toward me from the house's front steps. I barely recognized her without glasses and frump clothes. She actually looked quite delicious in a bright blue tube top and fashionably torn dark wash jeans, hair flying all over and just a touch of glossy lip stuff. "Will! You're here!"

Time to start acting.

"Hey, baby," I said, dropping my things and scooping her up in my arms to press a hard kiss on her lips. I didn't think I'd get into the physical thing so quickly with Clover…but after that first kiss in the coffee shop parking lot, I'd been looking forward to a second. Her lips were pure satin, with just a hint of something minty. And when they parted just a bit, she tasted even sweeter.

I stole a glance at the staff guy, who stood there watching in that nonjudgmentally-judgmental way that people who were paid to have no opinions, had.

Clover turned to him. "I'm good now, Sanders. Please handle the bags."

Sanders just stood there.

But Clover took my hand anyway, and went back to acting.

"How long did it take to get here? Was the traffic okay?" she asked, a little too cheerfully.

"Great drive. Got here in record time."

As if I went to Santa Barbara all the time.

Walking on the crunchy gravel driveway, I followed her into the massive mission-style house, which opened into a huge foyer overflowing with massive flower arrangements. But even better than the foyer were the jeans clinging to Clover's ass. I noticed a frayed spot right on her hip, a glimpse of lightly tanned flesh from her ass peeking out, and my cock twitched. Not to mention the way her tube top let her tits bounce when she walked—I was going to need some relief very soon, even if it were by my own hand.

When I'd met her, she'd been wearing what I guessed were 'teacher clothes.' Baggy, nondescript stuff that probably took a beating at the hands of little kids. But now her figure was on full display right in front of me, and without sounding like a scumbag, I had to say what I saw before me was really fucking something.

Actually, even better than that.

Her ass was a perfect, upside down heart, and her long hair swung down her back. I had no idea where her glasses had gone, and when she bent to introduce me to the family dog, I got a glimpse of a lacey tattoo on her lower back.

Booyah.

Now, I knew the girl had a wild side. No one could look as square as she did, and *be* equally as square. They said it was the quiet ones you had to watch out for...

"This place is really something," I said, looking around while following Clover's hot behind. A stairwell curved up to a wrap-around landing leading to several long hallways from what I could see.

"Oh, yeah, thank you. My sister and I grew up here."

We passed through a kitchen where a couple women were cooking. Because we didn't stop to say hello to them, I assumed they were 'staff' like Sanders.

"So does that mean this will all be yours one day?" I

asked with a laugh.

She turned to look at me, and lowered her voice. "Not really my style."

I could see that.

After the kitchen, we passed through a door and were back outside. There was a perfectly landscaped yard directly behind the house, and to the right, a huge infinity swimming pool overlooking the ocean. While I was taking it all in, I realized Clover had turned left, toward a series of small cottages.

I caught up with her. "What are these, hobbit houses?"

She smiled, and damn if that wasn't cute as hell. "Ha, funny. Something like that. My parents have these little cottages on the property for guests and such. I grabbed one for us. Better than my old room for sure."

That removed a thousand-pound weight from my shoulders. This was going to be tricky enough without sharing a bedroom across the hall from someone's parents.

"Cool, we've got our own pad," I said. I wished I'd kept that thought to myself with the look she threw over her shoulder.

I followed her into an unlocked, luxurious space with exposed beams, hardwood floors, overstuffed sofa and chairs, and large curved windows opening to flowers and other greenery. The bedroom held a four-poster bed with the thickest comforter I'd ever seen.

"I'll sleep on the sofa so you can have the bed," I offered, looking around. I spied my bags and wondered just how fast that guy Sanders had moved—we hadn't exactly wasted time getting there. "Whatever you're most comfortable with," I added. Although I knew what I was hoping for...

"Um, that might be a good idea. Hope you don't mind," she said apologetically.

"Give me a blanket and pillow, and I can sleep anywhere," I said, looking around the cozy room, disappointed. But hey, she was the client.

I peeked my head into a bathroom with a double-headed shower that looked like it could blast the paint off my Jeep if turned up high enough, and a deep walk-in soaking tub with jets...actual jets. Like a Jacuzzi. Even Zenia and Player would find this 'cottage' luxurious.

When I turned back to Clover, I found she was standing with her hands shyly clasped in front of her. "Will, everyone's meeting at the pool for a swim, and later, lunch."

Worked for me. Maybe I could get some laps in.

She reached into a dresser and pulled out a bathing suit, so I fished one out of my duffel.

We stood there, awkwardly staring at each other. Damn, was that a bathing suit in her hand or a tiny pile of scrap fabric?

"Would you mind turning your back while I change?" she asked.

I was glad she'd addressed that. I mean, I was ready to drop trou. Guys didn't really care that way. But something told me to follow her lead. Glad I'd waited.

"Not at all. I'll change too, then." Christ, I felt like I was in sixth grade gym class when you have to change for the first time in front of a bunch of other kids, and it was embarrassing as hell.

I watched her turn, and then I turned to face the wall behind me. I peeled off my shirt and let my pants fall to the floor, where I kicked them into a corner along with my boxers. I pulled up my swim trunks and was about to turn around when I stopped.

Were we going to go through this all weekend, turning our backs when it was time to dress? Well, like Zenia and Xander had said, anything sexual was optional, and it seemed Clover's interest in that sort of thing might not be there, despite the searing kisses we'd swapped.

"You ready?" I asked, still facing the bedroom wall.

"Um, just give me a sec." Stretched fabric snapped into place behind me. "Okay. Ready."

I turned to find her in a little white cover-up, slipping her feet into flip-flops, presumably with a bathing suit underneath.

"Wow. Look at all those tattoos," she said, looking me up and down.

I looked down at my arms and legs. "Oh yeah. I don't even notice them anymore."

She continued staring.

"Uh, are they a problem? I forget not everyone sees them as works of art," I said. Truth be told, I didn't really care. My tattoos were part of me, and if someone didn't like them, tough shit.

"Oh, no. They're great," she giggled nervously.

"Yeah?"

"Totally. No problem. I mean, I have one, too," she said.

"Oh really? Where?" I asked, playing as if I hadn't just been drooling over hers.

"Right here, she said, patting her lower back. "So, let's go. There are towels by the pool."

I knew I'd forgotten something. "Hey, before we go, how did we meet?"

"Oh, right." She sat down on the edge of the bed. "Geez, I almost forgot. Yeah, we need to get our stories straight. So, how about this—we met at a grad student party and have gone out a few times? Nothing serious, but we are having fun. That way if there's any mistakes, we can sort of play it off?"

"Works for me."

"All right. Shall we go for a swim?" she asked.

"Lead the way."

We followed a perfectly landscaped path lined with the same crunchy gravel as the driveway, and when we rounded a corner, found the gathering in full swing. Sanders, who was obviously pretty versatile, was working the grill cooking something that smelled damn good.

As we approached, Clover took my hand and pulled me toward a couple lounging near the pool. "Will, I'd like you to meet my sister, Jessamyn Lufkin, and her almost-husband, Robert Van Newsom."

Jessamyn, the exact opposite in appearance from her

sister with bobbed blonde hair and a slight figure, must have loved Clover's introduction. She just about doubled over laughing, while Robert, shorter than me by several inches, and basically nondescript, extended his hand, looking my tattoos over.

"You got some serious tats going on there, my friend," he said in a way that clearly passed judgment on me even if he wasn't going to say it. "And I thought I was bold, putting my fraternity letters on my ankle."

Was he serious?

"Yeah, that's some badass work," I said with a laugh, looking down at the tiny Greek letters that looked like someone had drawn with a Sharpie. *You wanna play alpha dog, buddy? That's fine by me. Humiliate yourself all you want.*

The smile faded from his face about as fast as he probably spent his father's money.

Sensitive fucker. Probably more used to being the 'big man' by default due to his name than anything else. And I did not give a shit. I'd proven myself plenty of times. I didn't care if your name was Jones, Smith, or if you were the Duke of York.

To escape, I looked across the pool to where Clover was laying towels on chairs for us. She'd taken her cover-up off, and I knew that if I didn't get in the water pretty damn fast, I'd be sporting a huge hard-on for the group. That wouldn't do. Not at all. Well, at least it'd prove I thought she was hot as fuck...but that didn't need to be broadcast for everyone to see.

So I dove right in.

CHAPTER 5

CLOVER

I had to give Hen some serious props for telling me about Player.

Will could not have been a better date that afternoon if he'd been a *real* date. In fact, I found myself wishing more than a couple times moments he *were*.

But he wasn't.

I nearly fell over when I got a glimpse of him in his swim trunks. Actually, that hadn't been my first glimpse of him nearly naked.

When we'd been changing, I turned to make sure he wasn't looking.

He wasn't.

But I did see him drop his pants to the floor. And the taut muscled globes of his ass practically jumped as he adjusted himself, a shadow of what I imagined he sported on the other side. My mouth was suddenly very dry.

I didn't feel badly for sneaking a peek. I mean, when I finally took off my bathing suit cover-up out at the pool, he was checking me out like there was no tomorrow. And while I was surely no supermodel, I could rock a bikini thanks to my small waist and big booty.

What was even better was when he met my parents. Mom, in her usual black maillot and huge straw hat, had grilled him only a few questions' worth when my dad had stepped in, offering him a scotch. Then Dad, in his Boston Red Sox hat, led him off on a walk, indicating points of interest on the property and beyond. That was my dad, always rescuing young men from Mom's grilling, calling it the 'Lufkin Inquisition' if he'd had a few too many scotches.

All was well, even when my dickish soon-to-be brother in law felt free to comment on Will's tattoos.

Whatever. I never liked him anyway, and he was clearly threatened by Will, even though Will had been nothing but a perfect gentleman.

"Hey," I said to Will once we were back in the cottage. "I'll probably take longer than you to get ready. Why don't you shower first, and then you can hang out in the library with Dad?"

"You sure?" he asked, turning to me with a towel around his shoulders.

I nodded, doing my best to keep my eyes off the bulge in his swim trunks.

While he ducked into the bathroom, I took the opportunity to peek inside his huge canvas duffel. I mean, I didn't reach inside and snoop around. No, I just pulled it open a bit further and peered inside.

Typical guy stuff. Nothing interesting, although I did note that a lot of it looked newish. Suddenly, his phone rang from inside the bag. I wasn't about to answer it, but I just so happened to see the screen. Accidentally of course.

A call was coming in from someone named 'Chili.' What kind of name was that? Was she a client? A girlfriend?

And why did I give a shit?

"Wow, great shower. It's all yours now," he said, emerging from the bathroom with a fluffy white towel wrapped around his waist.

Oh. My. God. Adonis himself, carved in the flesh with just a towel wrapped around his waist and a fraction of naked hip slipping out from where his thigh muscles spread the cotton open.

"Oh, glad you liked it. I'll meet you inside in a just a bit. Make yourself at home, okay?" I said, shutting myself into the bathroom, my heart hammering in my chest.

Had he seen me looking at his phone? Shit. I sat on the edge of the tub until I heard him leave, and could relax. It was more stressful being with such a handsomely dark man than it was spinning a huge tale about how I'd met him and we were hanging out together.

When I was finally ready, I went into the house and headed for Dad's library. As I got closer, I heard Jessamyn chatting Will up. I stopped in the doorway to watch, in the little shadow that I learned long ago gave me a spot to spy from without being noticed unless someone looked directly at me.

My pulse pounded in anger as I saw Jessamyn's hand running up and down Will's arm. "You are strong, aren't you, Will? And so fit. I mean, Rob was never like this."

She squeezed his bicep, and something like rage tore through me, not so much because he was my date, but because my sister would flirt with someone who, for all she knew, really might have been my boyfriend.

"Hey, guys," I said, busting right in on their little party.

Jess yanked her hand back to her side. Will just looked amused at both her flirting, and my reaction to it.

"Where's Dad?" I asked.

"Oh, um, he ran out to get some more scotch."

Will jiggled the ice cubes in his glass and winked.

Something about that helped settle me. It silently told me he was on my side.

I liked that.

I walked up to Will and took his free hand, entangling my fingers with his. "Since Dad's out, want to go for a little stroll? I can show you more of the property."

"Sure, baby," he said, and bent to kiss my temple.

We walked out without even looking at my sister, and that meant the world. In fact, since I'd entered the room, his gaze had never left me.

"Damn, what was that?" I asked Will as soon as we were outside. "Was she hitting on you?"

He shook his head. "I don't know, you tell me. You came along just in time. I was trying to think of a way to politely shake her off. Christ, can you imagine if what's-his-name had wandered in? That would have been a mess. He's such an insecure little fucker."

"Ah, you noticed, did you," I said laughing. But I did have to wonder for a moment if there was something going on between Rob and Jess that I hadn't noticed? "Well, sorry 'bout his snarky tattoo remark. He thinks he's so cool because he put his frat letters on his ankle."

"Eh. Who cares," he said. "I've met a lot of guys like him. And it always seems that frat letters tend to spell out giant, flaming douche regardless of the dude."

Good lord, this guy was chill.

"Well, he's used to being the only guy around, that is, besides my dad. Then you entered the picture today and, well, you are way more buff than he is. And stuff."

Ugh. Diarrhea of the mouth. *Shut up now.*

"Wait. Unless you liked her. Did you like my sister?" It wasn't like I owned Will.

And just as I began to look up at him, he reached for my chin and brought his face close to mine.

Ohmygod, ohmygod. The way his eyes burned into my face, the way he looked at me... If this was a fantasy, I was very, very close to immersing myself in it for at least the moment.

"I'm here for *you*, Clover. No one else. And I will make that very clear to everyone we see this week."

His lips were inches from mine, and I could no longer breathe. *Take me...I need it.*

But instead, he pulled back. "Now, show me the rest of this place. It's just insane," he said, taking my hand as we walked along a trail behind my parents' house.

Goddammit. I thought I was in for a kiss or two. Instead he'd smiled gently, like he knew what I was thinking, but was still taking charge...regardless of who was paying the bill for the week.

I wanted to scream, but I led him along the path my dad's gardener had built, the ground crunching under our feet. I pointed out the native California greenery I'd been taught about when I was a kid. I needed something to think about besides my raging hormones.

It turned out to be a great hour...strangely just like a real first date.

"Well, there you two lovebirds are," my dad bellowed as Will and I got back to the house and settled into Dad's library.

What had started out years ago as an escape for my father from his household of females had morphed into a hangout for the entire family. Over time, we'd used the media room less and less, which had a giant T.V. and tons of cushy seating, and just hung in the library when we wanted to be together.

"Dad, I think Jess and Rob are the lovebirds, here, don't you?" I asked.

He laughed. "Of course they are. I mean, they're tying the knot in—" He looked at his watch. "—T minus two days. But you guys look happy as clams. It's nice to see."

Guess we were pretty good actors.

And from the looks of Jess and Rob, they could use some lessons. How did two people about to get married end up looking so miserable together? They entered the library and took seats at opposite ends of the sofa, barely looking in each other's direction.

Yeah, there was something up with those two. But at that moment in time, it was not my problem. I had to get through the next several days convincing everyone Will and I were happy together, if not wild about each other.

And from what I could tell so far, it looked like things were going to go quite well.

"So, what do you kids think about taking a ride over to the Owenses' winery? I called ahead and they said they'd stay open late for us."

I took a quick peek at Will, and he looked game.

"That sounds like a great idea, Dad. Jess, what do you say?" I asked.

My sister nodded, slightly cheered. "Yes, let's do it, although you know I'm only having a tiny taste. Let me go see if Mom's ready yet." She bolted out of the room and up the stairs.

In the sudden absence of my sister, all eyes turned to Will, who seemed to command the room without even trying.

"So Will, tell us about yourself," Rob said, still miffed about his earlier showdown.

Uh-oh. Trouble was in the air. I just knew it. Will was clearly the natural alpha of the two, but Rob wasn't ready to give up his spot in the pecking order just yet and was spoiling for a way to come out on top.

So glad I wasn't a dude.

But Will was cool as a cucumber. He moved over to the edge of the ottoman where he sat just next to me, and put his elbows on his knees.

"I grew up in the San Fernando Valley, where I am now living with my little sister. I hope to finish my degree next semester," he said.

"The Valley? Really?" Rob said, sneering.

God, my future brother in law was an ass.

"Yup. The Valley. My parents recently died, so I'm taking care of my younger sister, Chili."

Chili was his sister? A weight lifted off my shoulders, and I felt ashamed for having even wondered earlier. Although…Chili? It was actually kinda cool.

"You know, Will, I have to admire a man who steps up to the plate when things get rough. Shows real character. I'd like to toast Will." Dad raised his glass, and of course Rob and I followed.

"To Will," Dad said.

Rob looked like he was going to explode. There he was,

trying to knock Will down, and instead was being shown up by someone who didn't even need to try. That must have sucked.

Too bad for him.

"Thank you, Mr. Lufkin."

"Will, don't call me Mr. Lufkin, call me Hart. Short for Hartwell," Dad bellowed. All his years around jets had left Dad a tad bit hard of hearing. He was always was a few decibels louder than he needed to be.

Before Rob could hurl another attack at Will, the sound of heels approached, and everyone turned toward the door as my mother swanned into the library with Jess right on her heels. Mom was overdressed for wine tasting, in floaty white palazzo pants and a matching silk blouse, but what else was new? The woman got dressed up to go grocery shopping, which never failed to amaze me.

"Thank you for waiting, everyone. Sometimes it takes this old girl a while to get her pretty face on." She tossed her hair back with a laugh.

We laughed, too. Why not?

Jess was our designated driver. Since she'd decided to starve herself into oblivion to make a more beautiful bride, she'd given up alcohol.

"The sacrifices one has to make," she'd told me.

Gag. She already looked fine, and quite frankly at that point was looking more starved than thin.

Will and I climbed into the way back of the van my dad had rented to shuttle people around for the wedding, and as we pulled out, he draped an arm around my shoulders.

I couldn't lie. It felt damn good. Like something I could get used to.

But I couldn't. He wasn't my boyfriend.

"I've never been to a winery," Will said, leaning toward my ear. "Any hints?"

He smelled so good.

"Oh, you'll love it. It's beautiful there, and the wine is really tasty," I reassured him. "Just relax and you'll enjoy yourself."

"Just like you." He gazed at me so hard I could barely breathe.

Damn. The guy knew how to work it.

And thank goodness it was getting dark, because I think I blushed from head to toe.

Because my parents were friends with the Owenses, they broke out all kinds of amazing reserve wines they saved for VIP visitors. 'Course, my parents had bought all the wine for Jess's wedding from them, *and* their entire family was on the guest list. They could spare a few bottles.

In their gorgeous winery with a soaring slanted roof and stone floor, they served us one taste after another—oaky chardonnays, rich cabernets, peppery zinfandels, and some of their very expensive pinots, which were all the rage in that part of California.

"Do they just keep pouring us wine? I mean, how many

do they have back there?" Will asked, leaning close to my ear again.

"I think they're wrapping up now. There might be one more to try. They always do the whites before the reds. I think they're serving port next. That's what they usually close with."

I don't know what it was—a combination of nervousness, or maybe happiness that a hot guy was paying attention to me—but all the wines the Owenses served us were amazing. And I probably tasted way more than I should have because when I went to go outside to get some fresh air, Will had to grab my arm to steady me as I stumbled over nothing.

"Where're you going, babe?" he asked, as I pulled ahead.

My dad smiled. Mom just looked confused.

"Um. Need some air," I said, heading for the door.

"Hey now. Let me take you," he said. Holding my elbow carefully, he led me outside, where he helped me remain on balance while I took some deep breaths. "Are you all right?" he asked. "Don't need me to hold your hair or anything?"

I giggled, shaking my head. "Now that's when you know it's good…the guy will hold your hair for ya. No, I'm okay. I just had a tiny bit too much wine. Need some fresh air." I looked up at the gazillions of stars in the evening sky. God, I loved Santa Barbara.

"Your dad suggested we go back to the house and watch a movie. What do you think?" he asked.

"That sounds great."

We said our goodbyes and thank-yous to the Owenses

and rounded up my parents. Jess and Rob were nowhere to be seen, until we'd gotten back to the van. There they were, sitting in the front seats and looking like two cats ready to tussle. The moment they saw us, they both went silent.

Something was going on. And it didn't look good.

"Okay, Jess, let's head home," Dad said, helping Mom into the van. "Time for a movie. What do you all think of *Apocalypse Now?*"

The car filled with groans.

"Dad, you always want to watch that movie," Jess whined.

"Well, I happen to think it's the best movie ever made," he said.

"Sweetie," my mom said to Dad, "it is a great movie. But probably not for tonight."

"Okay, fine. We can watch whatever you want, as long as it's not that *Pray, Eat, Whatever* movie again."

All the women in the car giggled. Poor Dad had been forced to watch that movie more times than any man should have.

On the short ride home, Will wove his fingers through mine again, and I leaned my head against his shoulder. I must have dozed off, because next thing I knew, he was shaking me.

"Guess you better take Sleeping Beauty to her room, Will," my dad said. "She can catch movies tomorrow."

"I think you're right."

Okay. I was tired, and I was buzzed. But I wasn't out of my mind.

When we got to the cottage, surrounded by the shrill call of crickets looking for mating partners, Will pushed open the door for me. "Well, should I drop you here and go join the family for the movie? Or would you like me to stay?"

"Um, well, could you come sit with me for a few minutes?" I asked. For some reason, the idea of Will watching something with everyone else while I was laid out seemed pathetic.

"Sure. Love to." He followed me into the cottage, and I flipped the lock on the door. I plopped down on the bed and patted the space next to me. "Join me?"

He lay next to me on his side, head propped on one arm. "How do you think we're doing?" he asked.

I was about to ask him the same thing.

"Pretty damn good, from what I can tell. Loved how my dad shut Rob down when he commented on your being from the Valley."

He nodded. "He's a good guy, your dad. You're lucky."

"I do feel lucky. It must be awful, having lost your parents."

He looked away, unable to meet my gaze. "Yeah. It is."

And in the next moment, his lips were on mine. His kiss was electric, strong, and powerful just like his others, but this time his hand rested on my side, and I leaned into him, wanting to feel his hand move up...or down...or anywhere, really. Just somewhere that would take things to the next level. I couldn't help whimpering when he pulled back. "Well, I better get to the movie."

"No!" I half howled, ready to grab his shirt if he so much as moved.

He rolled to his back and burst out laughing. "I was kidding. I'm not going anywhere."

So I cuffed his shoulder. "Jerk."

"Oh, I'm a jerk now. Okay then, I *do* think I want to join family movie night. I love that *Pray, Eat, Whatever* chick flick." He started to get up.

But before he could, I threw my arms around his neck and pulled him to me for a long, deep kiss.

As his tongue tickled mine, his hands traveled under my T-shirt and pushed up my bra. When his fingers landed on my sensitive nipples, I arched into him, begging for more touch.

I released him to pull my clothes off.

"Hey, hey, what's the rush?" he asked.

Huh?

I halted. "What do you mean?"

He reached for my hand. "You've had a bit to drink, and you're tired. Let's take it slow."

Did guys really do that? Take it slow?

"Come here," he said, taking my hand.

He lay me back on the bed, kneeling over me, and whipped off his shirt. He pulled off my half-removed shirt and bra and bent down to kiss my nipples.

Fuck this *slow* business.

But hey, if that's what he wanted, the way he was already making me feel was more than worth it.

His lips traveled down my stomach until he reached my

denim skirt. With his gaze locked on mine, he opened my fly and started to shimmy the skirt down over my hips, leaving me in nothing but a black, lacy thong.

"Mmmm. Such a beautiful girl." He ran his fingers over my pussy, through my panties, tickling me until I squirmed, my soaked panties clinging to my skin. He knew just where to stroke me without speeding things up too much. I moaned, desperate.

If he didn't rip those things off me soon, I would. And I might strangle him with them for teasing me.

Instead, he ran a finger just inside my waistband and then along the leg opening. When he got closer to my crotch, he slowed down, then reached in a bit further to brush the outside of my lips.

"Oh, you've shaved. Good girl," he said, pushing aside the crotch of my thong and lowering his mouth to my sex. "I'm hungry."

Just that bit alone had me ready to explode, but when he gently parted my lips and flicked my clit with his tongue, it took about three seconds to come.

I bucked my hips up to his mouth, and when he saw how close I was, he went to town by creating a suction with his lips and pulling my hard clit into his mouth.

That was all I needed. I began to pound the bed, my head thrashing. I tried to control my moans, but in the moment I wasn't sure how successful I was.

And I didn't care.

"Fuck, Will, I'm coming. Oh god, yeah," I murmured.

As the orgasm rolled over me, he parted my lips further and licked me from one end of my slit to the other.

"I had to taste you. And you're so good, baby." He moved up and lowered his mouth to mine to share my tang.

I took his hand. "That was amazing," I said dreamily.

He moved off the bed, and when I opened my eyes, he'd removed his clothes and was climbing in next to me.

"This okay? My sleeping here?" he asked me.

"I wouldn't have it any other way," I said and drifted off to sleep.

CHAPTER 6

WILL

With Clover asleep from a busy day of swimming, wine tasting, and pretending I was her boyfriend, I sneaked out of the cottage to call my little sis. I was pretty bushed myself, but needed to know Chili was keeping it together before I could get any shut eye of my own.

I was hoping for no more joyrides and no more arrests.

"Hi, Will," she said, answering on the fifth ring.

I did not take that as a good sign.

"Whatcha doin'?" I asked.

"Oh, cleaning and stuff," she said breezily.

I knew what breezy answers meant. No teenager in her right mind cleaned anything at eleven o'clock. If ever.

"Oh yeah? Cleaning what?" I asked.

"Um, cleaning the house. You know."

Oh, Christ.

"Chili, what are you talking about? You've never cleaned before."

"Are you saying you don't believe me?" she asked in that tone of righteous indignation that teenagers pull off so well.

"No, I didn't say that. What I did ask was what you were cleaning."

She harrumphed loudly. "If you don't believe me, you can just say so."

All right, that was enough of this 'tude. "If you don't want to tell me, I can ask Mrs. Jones to stop by the house to take a look."

"Will, I swear!" she whined.

"I need you to keep it together, Chili. You promised you would." I sighed and looked at the stars overhead. I was going to get this kid to shape up if it killed me.

"I know, Will. Could you please stop saying that all the time? I know I made a mistake the with car."

"Chili—"

"Oh, Will, I almost forgot. Your work friends, those other bodyguard guys, stopped by. They are so nice!" she said.

Way to change the subject.

"Sandy and Richard?" I asked.

I'd only just met the guys at Player, but when I'd told them about my situation, they offered their help. Freaking stand-up guys, if you asked me. I barely knew them and they'd signed up to tolerate a sixteen-year-old girl.

"Yeah, those guys. How is it that all you bodyguard

types are so hot? Especially that gay one. God!" Chili's voice had morphed from one of teenage bitchiness to downright enthusiasm. The transformation was amazing.

Bodyguards? Oh, right. That was the BS story I'd given her. I had to work harder to keep all my lies straight.

"Um, yeah. Coincidence, I guess. What'd you guys do?"

"They brought me some really legit Thai food and hung out for a bit. Then they had to go to work or something like that. Guess they had some famous people to protect."

Something like that...

"But they were so fun. Did you know Richard lives with his mother? He has to take care of her. Isn't that the sweetest thing?"

Holy shit. I hadn't known that. The guy had his own challenges but had time to help me with mine? Maybe there was more to being a member of Player than just the pay and spending time with women like Clover.

"They're soooo nice. Could we have them over again, sometime?" she asked.

"Yeah, sure. I mean I think they're pretty busy, but we'll schedule something."

While Chili blathered on about the guys, I wandered around the property, listening to the coyotes in the distance, marveling that life had once been so simple and that in the blink of an eye, boom. Life as we knew it ended.

I'd gone from being a carefree college student, just finishing up my degree thanks to a swim team scholarship, to burying my parents and arguing with judges who would decide the fate of my kid sister.

But feeling sorry for myself was not my style. I was going to make shit happen if it killed me.

I heard some voices nearby and knew I had to wrap things up. "Hey, Chil, I'm gonna let you go. I need to get back to work, okay? Will you let me know if you need anything?"

"Yes, *Will*," she said petulantly. "Bye!"

I headed back toward Clover's cottage when the voices got louder, and it became clear it wasn't a particularly pleasant conversation. Even though I knew better, I took a few steps toward the voices when I realized they were coming from a cottage on the edge of the property.

Note to self: the little places were not very soundproof. And Clover definitely didn't mind telling the world how much she liked what I did with my tongue. But I wasn't hearing Clover. It was her sister…and the douchebag.

"Oh Rob, would you just get over it…" Jessamyn said, slightly muffled.

He harrumphed. "You didn't have to act like such a little slut, throwing yourself all over that dirtbag from the Valley…" Rob said.

Okay. Apparently I was the *dirtbag from the Valley*. Maybe I could put that on my resume.

Jessamyn continued in a taunting voice, "Baby, I can't help it. Some guys are hunky, and some are, you know, skinny. Like you."

Christ. She knew how to hurt a guy.

I stepped on a snail shell that crunched loudly. Shit. The last thing I needed was to have the family think I was some sort of creeper. Rob would probably say I was casing the joint to rip them all off later.

But from the sound of the rustling inside the cottage, they appeared to have noticed nothing.

"Baby," Jessamyn said in a sticky-sweet voice, "you know I don't like rough-around-the-edges guys, like my sister does. I like *you*. Want me to show you how much?"

Hmmm. Not only was I *the dirtbag from the Valley*, I was also *rough around the edges*. I needed to work on my acting skills, apparently.

But hey, at least I was Clover's type. Nice of Jessamyn to throw that in there.

I hadn't thought of myself as rough, but I guess compared to this crowd, maybe I needed to smooth out the edges a little.

Actually, fuck that, and fuck them. I didn't need to do any of that bullshit. The sooner I got away from this crowd, the better. Well, scratch that. Clover and her dad were cool. Her mom was even sort of okay, even if she seemed a little self-absorbed.

Jessamyn continued sweet-talking Rob in a way that I guessed was their jam. I wouldn't give a twit like that the time of day—I mean, who the fuck puts down their part-ner?—but I had to admit, that when I heard them start to get it on, my dick got hard. Something about two annoying assholes completely unaware their probably shitty sex life was being overheard by *the dirtbag from the Valley* was hilar-ious. And also kind of hot.

"Mmmm, you're so naughty, Daddy," Jessamyn cooed. "You gonna lick my pussy now?"

"Yeah, bend over, little girl..." Rob groaned.

Oh Christ. They were into that daddy role-play bullshit.

My wood started to fade, and quickly.

I wandered back to my own cottage, amused as hell that I knew a bit more of what I was up against with those two idiots.

And of course, pleased with myself I'd gotten the beautiful Clover off. But now I had my own blue balls to deal with. Away from the bad role playing, my memories of Clover and her natural sexiness had my cock at full mast again, demanding attention.

I headed for the pool, which was covered by a thin layer of nighttime condensation as the heated pool water hit the cooler night air. I lay back on one of the lounge chairs and marveled at the peacefulness. With the big house now completely dark, I lay in the pitch-black of the night. It was all so freaking quiet after the noise and lights of L.A., and was really pretty goddamn amazing.

I reached my hand inside my shorts, and when I was convinced no one was around— and even if they were they wouldn't be able to see me in the shadows—I pulled out my cock. I imaged Clover's pretty mouth pistoning up and down over it, with her cute tush in the air and nice tits hanging down in front of me. In no time, I exploded into my hand.

I would rather have been with my pretty date, but

sometimes a guy just had to take care of business. I reached into the basket of used pool towels, wiped my hands, and then pushed the towel to the bottom of the bin.

I must have dozed off by the pool, because I woke up shivering and covered with dew. I wiped it off my face, and when I got my wits back, headed for Clover's cottage. I had no idea what time it was, but when I looked east, the sky behind the mountains was getting light. In the other direction, toward the ocean, the night sky was still black, the deep velvety black never seen in L.A. because of the lights. But out here, you could see the world the way it was created, and it was amazing.

I sneaked into the cottage and grabbed a hot shower to warm myself up. I carefully crawled under the down comforter and watched Clover snooze. She emitted a couple of cute girl-snores, and her eyes slowly opened.

"Hi," she murmured. "Is it time to get up?"

"No, sweetie." I smoothed her glossy hair back off her face. In spite of my initial concerns about being physical with a client, I was dying to kiss her again. But I'd wait till morning.

I could be patient when I wanted something. And Clover was someone I wanted very, very much.

Shit. For a moment, I'd forgotten I was being paid to hang out with the sweet girl, who, with all the privileges that surrounded her, was committed to being a school-teacher.

Even if I was only a fake date, I wondered how I'd gotten so lucky to have such an awesome fake girlfriend.

CHAPTER 7

CLOVER

God help me. I pushed my hair out of my face and tried to sit up in bed.

Was someone hammering my head? Because it sure felt like it. Christ, how much wine had I consumed at that stupid tasting my dad had arranged with the Owenses? Or had it really been that long since I tied one on?

Even with the sun was blazing between the slats of the cottage's shutters, I shivered in the morning chill, having fallen asleep buck-naked. To my delight, Will was right next to me. I snuggled into his warmth and realized there was something hard poking me in the back.

Oops. Busted.

I flipped over without waking him and lifted the covers just enough to see what I was dealing with.

Holy lord.

"Mmmm. Morning," he murmured, opening one eye. He turned and rolled over onto his stomach.

Damn.

But all was not lost. As soon as his breath returned to a steady rhythm, I lifted the comforter again.

Double damn.

Even on second inspection, his ass cheeks were freaking mountains of muscle. I mean, I'd seen them under his swim trunks the day before—both my sister and I had to force ourselves not to stare. When he'd emerged from the pool with the wet fabric clinging to him, little was left to the imagination. But to see his smooth skin up close and uncovered, well, it was like winning a jackpot.

I reached for a tuft of black hair that stood out from his bedhead, and he stirred again, flipping back over toward me, just missing my nose with a flailing arm.

Cripes, that would have hurt. But no harm done.

I continued stroking his hair until his eyes opened, and he greeted me with a smile that, if I'd not been lying down, might have knocked me on my ass.

"Hello, beautiful," he said quietly. "How'd you sleep?" He reached his arms up to stretch, flexing the hell out of his colorful tattoos.

"I slept pretty well for all that stupid wine I drank."

"You feeling okay?" he asked.

"Yeah. Wicked headache, but nothing that will kill me."

Lying on his side to face me, propping his head up on his hand and with his hair shooting in every direction, he was about the most beautiful man I'd ever seen. Certainly the most beautiful man I'd ever had in my bed.

Too bad he was a temp.

But at the moment he was mine, and I was his, and we were alone…

"I woke up, I think in the middle of the night, and you weren't here."

He laughed. "I was sitting out by the pool, and I guess I fell asleep. I woke up shivering and covered in dew."

I must have given him a horrified look because he said, "Don't worry. I took a quick shower before getting in bed."

"Oh, so you're a clean boy," I teased.

"Gotta be clean for my clean girl," he answered.

He reached for the sheet that covered my shoulder and slowly, slowly peeled it back, stopping only when it was lowered to my waist. I looked up at him from my pillow as he rolled me onto my back, lowering his mouth to mine.

His lips pressed mine, and god, were they firm. His tongue gently tickled me until I parted my lips, and he tasted me slowly and gently. I let my eyes flutter closed, losing myself as his fingers intertwined with mine and he pushed my hands over my head. He threw a leg over mine, pressing his very hard and very erect cock into my leg. I wanted to throw my own legs open in invitation, but held back.

Slow down, girl. You've got four more days of this all-you-can-eat hunk buffet, and he obviously doesn't mind giving you what you want.

Her lowered his mouth to my nipples, sucking one and

then the other, pulling hard until I cried out. I clutched at his hair with both hands and pulled him closer to me, that's how badly I wanted him.

"Beautiful. So beautiful," he murmured.

"Will?" I whispered.

"Yeah?"

"Will you lie back now?" I asked.

He looked at me with a question mark and slowly rolled back, his head propped on a pillow. I hovered over him, grasping his hard cock for the first time.

And what a beautiful cock it was. The tip glistened with precum, which I spread by running my hand down the shaft. He was so wide and thick through the shaft that my fingers would not close around him. But I continued over the head by widening my grip, and back down to his balls. Will closed his eyes, grimacing for a second. Sometimes things feel so good they actually hurt.

I positioned myself between his legs, and with my free hand, cupped his balls.

He sucked in his breath when I squeezed them lightly. "Fuck, baby, that feels so nice."

"Yeah? You like it?" I teased. I lowered myself to touch the tip of his cock with my tongue. It tasted so good I closed my lips around his head and created a suction that left him groaning.

"Goddamn. Easy, easy. I don't wanna come too fast." He stroked my hair as I pulled back to gaze at him. "I want to make it last."

I ran my lips down his shaft until he bounced against

the back of my throat. Tightening my hold on his balls, I pistoned my mouth over him faster, until he arched his back to drive himself all the way into my throat.

He grew even harder and suddenly exploded with loud groans, finally filling my mouth and flooding my tongue with his creamy, tangy seed. I swallowed it all, feeling sexy and powerful. When he was done, I licked him clean, nuzzling his cock until I let him slip from my mouth with an audible pop. I found him gazing at me with a big smile. He extended his arms in invitation, and I jumped into them, snuggling against his chest. I could have stayed there all day. No, make that all week.

And, I wasn't chilly any longer.

After breakfast, we all agreed to meet for some sun and a volleyball game in the pool. I'd never played with Rob, but my sister and I used to play for hours when we were kids. Will dove in and swam the entire length of the pool underwater and then back before emerging with a splash, shaking his hair out and grinning while the water glistened all over his muscled torso.

I guess you could do that when you were a swim team champ. And built like a god.

Deciding to relax some at first, I grabbed the lounge chair next to my dad. "Hey, Dad, got space for your baby girl?"

"Always," Dad said, letting me settle in. "He's a nice guy."

At first I wasn't sure who he was talking about, but then I saw him looking at Will. I looked around to make sure Jess hadn't heard. I didn't want any more drama in that department.

"Thank you, Dad. He *is* a nice guy."

He leaned a little closer. "Think you'll be keeping him around?"

My head snapped in Dad's direction. "What? Why do you ask that?"

He shrugged. "I don't know. I guess you don't usually keep guys around. This one seems like a keeper, though, and the attraction between you guys... Listen, it's hard for me to think of my baby girl as a woman, but I can see you're into him."

"Yeah? Well, we'll see." I was not a fan of lying to my father, but I smiled at him through feeling like a shit.

"I think your mom likes him, too," he said.

"Really? I thought all she wanted in the world is for me to date Nathaniel."

Dad rolled his eyes. "Yuck. I don't see you with that simpering creep. I don't know why your mother keeps pushing him on you."

I looked around to make sure Mom was nowhere in the vicinity. "She does it because his family is loaded. You know Mom. She's all about money. Always has been."

He looked down at the beer in his hand and nodded slowly. "Yeah. I know. I love your mother to death, but... that's her thing. Guess it's a side effect of those lean years before you were born, when we were building jets for the jet setters but not making checks like them. But you know, sweetie, she thinks she's doing what's best for you. Just keep that in mind."

Well, damn.

"Hey, Clover, let's play volleyball!" Will called out, laughing. "I need a teammate!"

I looked at my dad, who nodded. Before I jumped in the pool, I gave him a kiss on the cheek.

Jessamyn and Rob jumped in right after me.

"Shall we play boys against girls, or couple against couple?" I asked.

"Couples," Rob answered quickly.

I'd sort of hoped that Jess and I would play against the guys, but it was all good—at least I hoped so. I could see Rob already bristling again, ready to try and reassert himself.

"Dad," Jess called, "flip a coin to see which team starts first."

"Okay. Somebody call it," he said, throwing a coin in the air and catching it.

"Heads!" Jess yelled.

Dad opened his hand. "Heads it is. Jessamyn and Rob, you're up."

Jessamyn got in position to serve, and Will and Rob braced themselves. The ball sailed over the net, in my direction. I jumped to tap it, setting it up for Will, who smashed it into the water right in front of Rob.

"Hey, guys, it hit the net," Rob announced, and I inwardly groaned. Not this shit.

"Dude, it totally cleared the net. Sorry," Will said. His self-assuredness was freaking hot as hell, and it stung Rob even more when he saw that nobody was going to back him up on his claim.

Rob mumbled something under his breath and lobbed the ball over the net so I could serve. I sent it in my sister's general direction, but Rob jumped in front of her and hit it in Will's direction. Will was able to return it, before we realized Rob had elbowed Jess in the face in his haste for the ball, leaving her with a bloody nose.

"Rob, look what you did!" Jess shrieked.

Will jumped out of the pool at lightning speed, grabbed a towel, and brought it to my sister. Rob snatched it out of Will's hands and held it under Jess's dripping nose.

"C'mon, honey," my dad said, extending a hand to Jess to help her out of the pool. "Sit over here for a sec."

"Rob, you're such an asshole!" Jess screamed.

Whoa.

"It was an accident, Jess. For Christ's sake, I'm sorry."

I elbowed my way past Rob and put an arm around Jess. "Are you okay? It doesn't hurt too badly, does it?"

"Mmmm," Jess mumbled. "I'm fine. The bleeding has slowed," she said, pulling the stained towel away from her face. It was probably the pool water, but it still looked like someone had opened a gusher on my sister's face.

"Thank you for the towel, Will," she said, smiling at him.

And deliberately ignoring Rob.

Things were getting ugly.

"I'm going inside," Jess said. "I've had enough of the pool for one day." As she stood, Rob took her arm, which she forcefully flung off. She headed back to her cottage while the rest of us stood there, watching.

"Jessamyn," Will called, "are you sure you're okay—"

Suddenly, out of the corner of my eye, Will lost his footing and went down. When I'd turned to see what was going on, he was flat on the pool deck with a cut on his forehead.

"Will! Oh my god, are you okay?" I asked, rushing to him.

"Geez, you kids are a mess today," my dad said.

Will was back on his feet as quickly as he'd gone down.

"I'm fine, really." He shot Rob a dirty look, one with plenty of unspoken meaning.

Clearly, I'd missed something.

Blood trickled down his temple. What the hell had happened?

"Hey, let's go to the kitchen and get you cleaned up," I said, taking his elbow in a way that reminded me of how he helped me the night before.

We left Rob at the pool, smug written all over his nasty face.

Inside the kitchen, I grabbed the first aid kit the staff used and dabbed Will's head. The cut was nasty but not too deep. "Did Rob have something to do with this? I saw some looks being exchanged between you two. What's going on?"

He shrugged, his face clouding. "It's nothing."

Such a liar. Will might be more of a natural alpha than Rob, but that didn't mean he was going to just shrug off a cheap shot. If anything, it probably bothered him more to not react.

"Ha. I knew it! He totally had something to do with your wipeout." I reached for a band-aid, but Will held up a hand.

"No, no, I don't need that. I'm fine."

I threw the band-aid on the kitchen counter and went back to dabbing. "Why didn't you deck him? He's such an ass."

He steered me away from the staff working the kitchen and lowered his voice. "I'm here for you. Not my ego. And I'd never let a piss ant like that get under my skin, anyway."

"Well. Thank you."

"I want to help you get through this wedding," he continued, quietly. "I have no intention of making you look anything less than perfect."

I stood on my toes to kiss him. "Next time, you have my permission to deck him."

Not that he needed my permission for anything.

"Be careful what you wish for," he said grimly, touching the cut on his head. "Because I think I'm going to have the opportunity."

CHAPTER 8

WILL

"Will, grab a seat here, my friend," Hart bellowed from across the restaurant's private dining room.

I pulled a chair up to the table where Rob, a few of his friends, and Hart had gotten a head start on their men's night out in a swanky Santa Barbara restaurant.

Hart Lufkin. One of the coolest people I'd met in a long, long time.

Aside from his daughter, of course. Hart was incredible successful but totally down-to-earth. From what Clover had told me, he'd worked hard to build the business his father had started, so while he enjoyed the fruits of his labor, he'd never forgotten what it took to get there.

"Thank you," I said, settling in while Hart slipped a fancy box toward me.

"Choose one, Will. We're all going to have a cigar. Hey, that cut on your head from earlier today cleaned up nicely."

"Clover did a good job. She should be a nurse," I said.

Speaking of which, I wished I was back at the cottage with her. Alone. And in bed. But Hart had invited me, and I wasn't about to insult his generosity.

I reached into the box, and Hart handed me a cutter. One of Rob's friends tossed me a lighter, and I fired up.

The guys started sharing college fraternity stories when Hart turned to me. "Thanks for joining us tonight, Will," he said.

"Well, thank you for including me."

"You're welcome. I hope you've been enjoying yourself. Maybe we can go out on my boat tomorrow?"

"That would be great. I'd love it." I wasn't usually a cigar smoker, but I had to admit, the ones these guys had were awesome, and while I'd never be one of those serious smokers…a couple times a year was just about right.

"So when do you think you'll be able to get back to school?" he asked.

"I'm hoping next semester," I admitted honestly. "I'm ready to be done. I had to take this semester off, but I swore I'd go back."

Hart laughed, nodding. "Well, I have to hand it to you, taking care of your sister and all. Although I have to admit to something…I've got USC season tickets."

Ah-ha. He was a supporter of the University of Southern California—UCLA's archnemesis in every way.

I laugh, shrugging. "Thank you, and I forgive you.

Although I really had no choice. Not that I didn't want to. My sister is a good kid. Generally."

Hart waved over the server for another round of some very expensive scotch. "You might not know this, but Clover was rebellious in her day. Actually, she still is, in her own way."

Rob's buddies were on to the topic of investing and the best places to put all the money they had. Wouldn't that be a killer problem to have?

"You know, Will," Hart said, ignoring the young blowhards and leaning closer toward me, "all I want is for my girls to be happy. And for my company to be able to build the best airplanes in the world. Everything else in life is gravy."

"How'd you get into the airplane business, Hart?" I asked, curious.

"My dad started the company from nothing. I mean, he started as a mechanic for one of the airlines when he was just nineteen years old, right out of a quick tech school. He worked his way up, went to work for one of the manufacturers, and then got enough investors to start his own company building private jets."

A slew of waiters emerged, one by one, from another room with trays of lobster tail and filet mignon.

"That's so cool. My parents were teachers. Just like Clover," I said.

He nodded as we filled our plates. "No kidding. No wonder you like her."

If he only knew.

He continued. "I went to work for my dad right out of college, starting as a sweep monkey on the fabrication floor. Worked my way up. Got no special breaks, I can tell you that. But I'd never considered doing anything else. It's what I'd always wanted. Now, I wish one of my girls was interested in the business, but Jessamyn recently quit working to get married, and you know Clover—she's completely committed to being an educator."

It was clear that Clover's decision in this area was a sensitive subject. But I wanted to know more. "Sounds like there's been some blowback for her over that decision. If you don't mind me prying?"

It was so odd that anybody would object to someone wanting to be a teacher, but it was a different world I was in at that moment. One I knew little about, apparently.

Hart nodded and addressed the topic with no hesitation. "We'd expected her to go into the family business and make a good living for herself. She's so smart, and she started in business before hitting us out of the blue with her decision to get her Master's in Education. It seems that aircraft's not her calling. I'm proud of her, although her mother leans on her to do something more...I don't know...lucrative. She's a piece of work, that one," he said.

"You mean Mrs. Lufkin?" I asked.

"Yes, Patsy. She's a little obsessed with the whole wealth thing. Wants her daughters married off to the right guys, that sort of thing. There were some...lean years. She hasn't forgotten them."

I laughed. "Well, then I guess I don't have to worry

about her trying to marry off Clover and me, then."

Hart turned pink. "Oh, I didn't mean to say that. It came out wrong."

I patted him on the back. "No offense taken, Hart."

I checked out Rob and his buddies at the other end of the table where they were plowing through scotch like it was a competition.

Hart saw me looking. "Yeah, those meatheads are gonna regret their drinking tomorrow, mark my words. A good scotch is like a good woman. She should be savored, sipped, and treasured. Not gulped, wasted, and tossed in the trash."

"Will," Rob called, "c'mon. Let me pour you some of the good stuff." He passed me a glass. "Bet they don't have stuff like this in the *Valley*, do they?"

His friends rolled their eyes at him.

"No, Rob, but we don't have assholes like you, either, so it's all good."

There was silence around the table as the smile faded from Rob's face, and then one of his friends burst out laughing. "Dude, he just smacked your ass *down*."

After a second, the other guys exploded in laughter, too, and Hart shook his head, politely trying to hide his own smile. Rob, on the other hand, looked like he wanted to deck me. For his sake, it was a good thing he didn't.

I was keeping things together for Clover, but a guy could only take so much crap, especially from a skinny weasel like Rob. He was inches away from limping down the aisle on his wedding day with a face covered in bruises.

I had no idea what Clover's sister was doing marrying him, but it wasn't my problem. In a few days I'd be saying *adios* to the whole gang.

And damn if that thought didn't feel like a kick in the stomach. I'd be lying if I didn't admit I'd be sorry to say goodbye to the lovely Clover. Honestly, if I'd met her on campus, I would have been on her hard core. Instead, fate had made me just a paid date...although a paid date with benefits. So I was going to make the most of the time I had left with her. That included not wasting any more time than I had to with Rob and his frat-boy friends.

"Now you see," Hart said as the guys continued to bust on Rob, "there are downsides to success and money. I have to deal with idiots like this. And in many ways, I know it's made my daughters' lives harder. Easier in some ways, and harder in others." He leaned closer. "You know what I mean, don't you, son?"

Um, yeah. Sure.

On my drive back to the house, I found I'd missed a call from Zenia. I pulled my Jeep over to the side of the road and redialed her.

She picked up on the first ring. "Will. How is everything?"

"Hey, Zenia. Things are going well, I think. It's a beautiful place, and Clover and I are having fun."

"Okay. Excellent. Glad to hear it. I appreciate your good

work," she said.

"My pleasure, Zenia."

Yes, it was a pleasure, truth be told.

"Clover is very...um...special." I didn't want to say too much, and Zenia hummed warningly.

"Don't get attached, Will. After this arrangement, you probably won't see her again. Contact with clients outside appointments is not permitted. But I think you know that."

If there was one thing I didn't like, it was being told who I could and couldn't be friends with.

Keep your eye on the ball, asshole.

"I understand, Zenia. I feel fortunate that we are having fun, is all. It would be tough to do this with someone you didn't click with, you know?"

Good recovery, right?

As if she were reading my mind, she asked, "How's your sister, anyway? I understand Sandy and Richard have checked in on her. They're all buddies now?"

"Yeah, can you believe it? They're her new brothers, second-in-command. Those guys are the real thing, I tell you."

I heard a door open and close on the other end of the line, and Zenia moved to end the call. "Okay, sweetie, I'm glad all is well. I need to go now, but if you need anything, you know where to reach me."

"See ya later, Zenia."

As I made my way up the drive to the Lufkin property, I dialed Chili.

"Hey, big brother," she said.

"Hey, kid. What are you up to? Keeping it clean, I hope," I said.

She sighed deeply. How the hell had my parents tolerated the teen drama?

"I'm *fine*. You know, you don't have to check up on me, Will," she said testily.

"I know I don't have to. I *want* to."

Silence, so I continued. "Chili, you should see this place in Santa Barbara where I'm working. It's amazing. Huge house up on a hill, swimming pool, guest cottages. The works."

"Wow. It sounds super nice," she said, semi-interested.

But I wasn't giving up easily. "It's a testament to what you can earn with good grades and hard work. The sky's the limit, really."

"Oh, I get it. You're trying to impress upon me that if I'm a good girl and study hard, I can have nice things, too," she said.

"You're right, Chili. I do want to help you see what life is like when you have options. When you're not hemmed in by circumstances."

"That's fine, Will...but can you do it without sounding like an after school special or a Lifetime teen drama movie? I get it."

The kid was too smart by half.

I parked and headed back toward the cottage, speaking quietly, although I wasn't sure anyone was around, anyway. "What have you been doing with yourself?" I asked.

"Well, I was hanging at Mrs. Jones's earlier. She helped

me with my English homework. Did you know how smart she is? I never knew she was a retired math *and* English teacher."

Neither had I, but I was not in the least surprised.

"That sounds good. And use that resource, bust your butt."

"I will... she cooks well, too."

Ah...the plot became clearer. "Okay, Chil, I gotta roll. You know how to reach me if you need anything, right?" I asked.

"Yes, Will, I know how to reach you. But I won't be needing anything. I can take care of myself just fine."

"Like the way you and your friends took that car and were busted? Yeah, I call that taking care of business," I said.

Another dramatic sigh. "You don't have to be so mean, Will," she said, her voice cracking.

Shit. When would I remember the bag of hormones thing Mrs. Jones had told me about? I had a lot to learn about this parenting shit, and not a lot of time to do it.

"You're right... Look, I'll do my best, you do your best, okay? Love you, Chil," I said as sweetly as I could. "I'll see you in a few days."

I ended my call and walked around the property, which I was happy to find deserted. Not even Sanders, the butler-guy, was around, and that guy seemed to be everywhere. All I could hear was a coyote howling in the distance, like he had a broken heart.

I had a feeling I might feel that way, too, in a few days.

CHAPTER 9

CLOVER

"Dad likes Will," Jess said. "He told me." She settled into a mani-pedi chair next to me and shook a bottle of wedding-pink nail polish. Seriously, that was the name of the color.

I hoped my sister realized my dad liking our guys was not a zero-sum game; just because he liked Will, didn't mean he liked Rob any less. Although with the way Rob had been behaving lately, anything was possible.

"He does like Will, doesn't he? I think he likes a man who's, um, making his own future."

Or something like that. I hated trying to think on the fly about it all.

"What's his story anyway? All I know is that he lives in the Valley, thanks to Rob's being an ass to him," Jess said.

"Well, he had to drop out of school with one semester to go because his parents died."

"That much I know. Anything else?" she asked.

Was she testing me? Trying to find out how much I knew about him?

I dipped my feet into the heavenly, swirling, warm water. The Zen-like ambiance of the day spa Jess had selected for us had already calmed me by a multitude of factors.

"Well. He's taking care of his younger sister." But I think she already knew that, too.

Jess leaned her head back in the cushy chair and closed her eyes. "Damn. That's a lot of responsibility. Can you imagine taking care of me if something happened to Mom and Dad when we were kids? We'd both have killed each other in a week."

"Hey, Jess, can I ask you something? Do you think Will and I seem overly attached? You know, do we hang on each other too much? I mean, I've wondered if we're too affectionate in front of everyone," I said.

Jess lifted her head from the chair, scrunching her face at me. "What? Mom and I were thinking you seemed kind of distant. Like you didn't know each other that well and maybe you weren't such a good match."

Okay, I was completely confused at that point.

"Really? Huh. Okay."

"Well, *do* you like him?" Jess asked.

Good question...

"Of course I do. I wouldn't have invited him otherwise."

I stared down at the wedding-pink polish that my sister was forcing on me. Normally, I preferred about the darkest color I could find.

And I hated lying to her.

But was I really lying? The honest truth was that over the past couple of days, I'd gone from meeting the guy to really wishing I'd come to know him the traditional way. I mean, he was going to UCLA at the same time I was, right? Why couldn't we have run into each other there?

Then again, his being on the swim team meant his schedule was vastly different from mine, and UCLA was huge. I might as well have wished I'd run into him because we lived in the same county.

But still… I knew inside that the line between professional 'satisfaction' and really liking Will was getting very, very blurred.

"Well, I wish Rob could be nicer to him. He's so damn jealous. He grew up with all the privilege in the world, and yet he's so insecure." Money bought a lot of things, but not everything.

I watched the first coat of paint go on my nails, which I'd be taking it off right after the wedding. I was just *not* a pink girl.

"I'm sorry he hasn't been nice," Jess agreed. "And Will is such a gentleman. You hang on to him—guys like that are anything but a dime a dozen."

A waif of a woman came into our room. "Ladies, your massage room is ready when you are."

Nothing beat a spa day. Well, except for a long morning in bed with Will.

I'd come home the night before from Jess's girls' gathering and found him sound asleep. He'd looked so handsome, lying there on his back with one arm stretched overhead. I felt a little stalker-ish, but I couldn't *not* watch him snooze, quietly and with the occasional snore.

Who knew snoring could be so sexy?

I was dying to trace a finger along the tattoo that covered his shoulder down to the perfect shock of hair in his underarm. I wanted to run circles around his dark nipples, and follow the line of hair that led to his belly button. I was impressed with my newfound self-restraint. A week ago I might have just jumped him the way he was and demanded immediate attention.

So far, my checking him out had not disturbed him; he'd remained sound asleep when I peeled the covers back to find his semi-erect cock resting across his lower abdomen, surrounded by a splay of pubic hair that was neither too light nor too heavy. His balls dangled between his spread legs, where another tattoo, tribal in nature, began at the top of his thigh and went to his knee.

Would it have been creepy to take a picture? God, I was tempted. But I didn't. I mean, shit, I wouldn't want anyone to take a photo of me without my consent.

So I continued my spying while getting ready for bed,

searing his image into my mind to last me the rest of my life if I had to. Then slowly and carefully, I slid under the coverlet that I pulled up over us both. As I turned to flip off the light, Will's hand landed on my thigh, sliding up to my breast where he pulled one of my nipples until my breath became ragged and pleasure zipped through me.

Somebody was no longer asleep.

In the pitch dark, he rolled me onto my back and ran his fingers through my hair, brushing his lips over my cheeks until he found my mouth. He'd pressed mine with such a passion, I'd wanted to spread my legs and let him do whatever he wanted without delay. I needed him, and I needed him right away.

While kissing me, his hand wandered along my stomach until it reached my pussy, which had been slick with excitement since I'd started spying on him. Two fingers parted my lips and made small circles on my hard nub until I bucked my hips, pressing into his hand and begging for more.

Without a word, he reached off the side of the bed—for what, I initially did not know. But I heard plastic tearing, and watching his silhouette against the moonlight sneaking between the shutters, saw him rolling on a condom.

He moved back between my legs, effortlessly placing my feet over his shoulders as if I weighed nothing at all, and lowered his hips between mine. I put my hands on his ass and slowly pulled him toward me. He notched himself at my opening, and I guided him inside me just an inch, my back arched and my body trembling.

All this, still, without a word. Well, except for a rasping purr of approval from me.

We froze, his cock just spreading me open as I gushed over his condom-sheathed hardness. It was so freaking crazy erotic, each of us knowing what the other wanted and needed so clearly that we needn't say a single thing. We were in perfect unison, our hips rocking together as he pushed the rest of the way inside my throbbing pussy. I clenched at his huge erection, and my hands roamed his hot, sweaty skin. Will pulled back, lowering his mouth to mine as he pushed inside again, our moans swallowed as he started thrusting in and out of me.

It wasn't going to be a quick thing, a rocket ship to a hard-hitting orgasm. Instead, Will and I worked together, drawing it out and making it last. He ground against me, changing his strokes to keep us both growing, like he was lighting up one part of my body before we worked together to light up another. It rolled through me, my stomach tingling, my breasts tightening and sending fire-works straight to my brain... Even my arms and legs started to pulse with the energy of our connection.

I slammed my head back against the pillow as the sensation that started building between my legs spread, leaving me shuddering from head to toe and so, so thirsty for air. Will began to pummel me purposefully, and I could feel his cock swell and his balls tighten, as we both knew we couldn't hold back this time. We didn't want to, and the groans he released as he came fired off my own explosion. My pussy tightened around him, and I shook with a pleasure I wished would never end.

As I came down, Will kissed me softly, chuckling. "Welcome back... I was hoping you'd wake me up."

"Mmmm, and what if this is a dream?"

"Then let's share it."

I wasn't sure whether I was asleep, dreaming, or just floating through the universe with Will's arms leisurely wrapped around me, but I didn't have another thought until my sister woke us by knocking on our door. Beyond the cottage's shutter slats, the blinding sun invited itself in.

What the hell time was it?

"Clover? Hey, it's time to go. The spa awaits," she'd called through our locked door.

"Oh my god. I'm sorry, Jess," I hollered, wondering just how I'd slept so long. "I'll be out in five."

Will, lying back in bed with a hand under his head and a big smile on his face, had watched me run around our room getting ready. He looked damn good, and for a moment I was tempted to blow my sister off.

"Maybe I'll wait here for you, ready to go for when you return," he said, wickedly. He smiled and waved from the bed, looking all gorgeous in his nakedness.

The temptation just about made me blow off the spa

day with my sister. "Very funny. Have some fun, go for a swim... I'll be back later."

He nodded, and that damn one-sided dimple was back.

~

"Hey, what's that on your neck?" Jess asked, smiling, as we settled into the massage room, our tables separated by a few feet.

My hand flew to my neck. "What? What do you mean?" I didn't feel anything.

"Ha, you dork. You have a hickey..." she sang.

"Oh, cripes. Well, what can I say?" I said, blushing to the roots of my hair. "I mean, I am seeing Will. Stuff happens, and I'm not a nun."

She jumped up on her massage table facedown and pulled the sheet to her mid-back. "Hey, at least you're having fun. Will's hot as hell. I'd be all over him, too. He's about a thousand percent better than The Jester. No joke."

I shivered, thinking of The Jester.

After a ninety-minute massage and an hour-long facial, it was fair to say we floated back to the car, clutching each other and our bottles of water. We'd been instructed to drink as much as possible to flush the toxins our treatments had surely released.

I didn't know a thing about toxins, but who were we to argue? When you felt that amazing, it was impossible to question anyone.

"Oh *shit.*"

I followed Jess's gaze.

Her car had a flat.

"Oh, boy," I said.

She began fishing through her purse. "Let me call Rob."

She got his voicemail. "Hey, baby, my car has a flat. Clover and I are at the spa. Can you come help?"

She studied the tire like it might change on its own. "Where the hell *is* that guy, anyway?"

I pulled out my phone. "I know who we can call."

Will showed up not ten minutes later in his Jeep, crossing the parking lot and planting a big kiss on my lips.

I could make a habit of getting flats, if he were to come to the rescue every time. Except in couple more days, I wouldn't have him to call.

"Hey, Jess, can you pop your trunk?" he asked as Jess giggled. "What?"

"I'm just thinking that if you asked, she'd let you pull up to her rear bumper," Jess teased, making Will roll his eyes. "Oh come on, I saw the hickey. I think it's cute."

I sat down on the curb to admire his flexing muscles as he pulled out the spare tire and tools needed to change Jess's flat. By the time he was done, he was a sweaty mess, his hands black with filth and a couple grease stains smeared across his T-shirt.

All I could think about was dragging him back to bed.

"Oh my god, Will, you saved the day. Thank you so much," Jess said. "I have no idea where Rob was." She beamed at him, and I had to admit, I did, too.

Christ, what had I done? Everyone liked him. *Especially me.*

"I have an idea," Jess said, clapping her hands together. "Will, why don't you go wash your hands, and we'll go to a casual lunch at the beach?"

"Oh my god, what a great idea, Jess," I said. "Are you in, Will?"

"Are you kidding?" he asked, nodding his head. "You think I would be stupid enough to pass on lunch with the two most beautiful women I've ever set my eyes on? Let's go."

We headed to a touristy place near the water where, to be honest, the food had never been all that great. But the views and ambiance were, and sometimes that's what the occasion really called for. Jess and I ordered huge salads, and Will got a burger with bleu cheese and bacon.

"So Will," Jess began after the waitress left, "when do you think you'll be back in school?"

"Well, if all goes according to plan—" He stole a look at me, probably because he was hoping I hadn't told a different story. "—I'll be back next semester. I need to get my kid sister situated first, though." He continued with the story of his business studies and how he'd helped his friends launch a successful food truck business.

I'd never dreamed he and my sister would be as engaged in conversation as he and my dad had been. It was like he was a family member.

But I reminded myself, that would never happen. It could never happen. I mean, at some point the truth would have come out, and explaining to my parents that I'd hired an escort and then sort of decided to keep him around? Yeah… Dad's cool, but even he might have shit himself on that one.

Still, I couldn't stop the fantasy from running around in my head all through lunch, and more than once Jess gave me the look that told me Will totally had her seal of approval. We were heading back to the car, Will and I hand in hand, when Jess realized her phone had been buzzing in her purse.

"Geez," she said, rummaging around in her bag. "I completely lost track of time, I was having so much fun with you two. I hope it isn't…oh, it was just Mom."

She tapped her phone a couple times and put it up to her ear.

In the meantime, I pulled Will around to the other side of the car. "Thank you for being so nice to my sis. I think it was good for her to just spend a little time with us. I hope we lowered her stress level."

"Hey, guys," Jess said the moment she swiped her phone closed, her stress level obviously back on high with her eyes tight and her keys in her hand. "We gotta go."

Her car beeped as she pressed *unlock,* and she jumped behind the wheel of her SUV, nervous about something.

"Jess, what's going on?" I asked, wondering if I should ask for the keys and demand to drive.

"Mom's been trying to reach us. I guess she got back from her bridge game and found Rob pacing back and forth in front of the house, half out of his mind. He didn't know where we were." She sped around several corners and up a hill, barely scraping through two red lights and completely blowing a third. "I gotta get back before he flips."

She dropped us at Will's Jeep, which we'd left at the spa, and screeched out of the lot, leaving us behind.

When we were alone, I laughed. I couldn't help myself. "I have to say, the thought of Rob freaking out, mumbling to himself, sounds hilarious."

I looked over at Will, who just sighed. "You know, I feel for that guy. He's a mess. An insecure mess."

"You got that right... Funny part is, compared to what you're dealing with, he's got one problem to your ninety-nine," I replied. "I gotta ask...are you embellishing any of it?"

Will shook his head, and inside of me my heart lurched again. We jumped in his Jeep and drove home, the whole time with me wishing the fantasy were real.

When we pulled up to the house, Jess and Rob stood in the drive out front. Rob gestured with his arms like a crazy man, pacing with Jess right on his heels.

"I'm sorry, baby," Jess pleaded as we exited Will's car, "we didn't mean to leave you out. I tried to call you, but you didn't pick up. And we were having so much fun, I didn't even hear my phone..."

Oops. *Not* the right thing to say.

"Great!" he said, throwing his hands in the air. "So glad you were having fun with another man." He turned and scowled at Will as we passed him on our way into the house.

"Dude, relax," Will murmured.

"*What did you say?*" Rob thundered.

"Nothing, man," Will said without even turning around.

Once inside, we ran smack into my mother. "Clover, may I have a word with you?"

"Sure, Mom." I turned to Will. "I'll meet you back at the cottage, okay?"

He planted a quick kiss on my cheek and happily escaped my family drama.

I followed Mom into the library. "Clover, what is it you are doing with that man?"

"With Will? What do you mean?"

She calmly pushed an invisible strand or hair from her smooth face. "He's...a bit rough around the edges." Her words might have been cutting, but her face was beautiful and sweet. She was skilled that way.

I put my hands on my hips. "What do you mean? Because he's not rich, like that psycho outside who is verbally abusing your daughter at this very moment? Or Nathaniel, who is completely lacking in character?"

"Clover, you know very well what I mean—"

"I *do* know what you mean, Mom. And I don't like it. At all." I turned on my heel to head back to the cottage, with Rob's loud voice filling the air, as he scolded my sister for, well, everything.

CHAPTER 10

WILL

I looked at my watch. I'd call Chili from the road.

Grabbing my duffel from the closet, and I began stuffing my belongings back into it. After listening to what Clover's mom said, I was getting the hell out of there. I didn't need to spend any more time with those people.

I'd overheard Clover's mom dogging me, and I'd had enough. Sure, Clover was great, and her dad was cool, but I didn't need the bullshit baggage that came along with their family. I had nothing in common with any of them and didn't need their snobby asses thinking they were better than anyone else.

And I was done walking on eggshells around that loser Rob. Who gave a shit whether he was loaded or not? The dude had no game whatsoever, and it was clear Jessamyn knew it. Maybe she was the kind who got her kicks out of making her man look weak, maybe she was trying to get him to stand the fuck up...or maybe in five years she'd be dumping his sorry ass. I didn't really care. I needed to get the hell out of Dodge before I showed him what a real man was made of.

Just as I finished stuffing my shirts into the bag, my phone buzzed with a text from Chili.

Hey bubba!

I took a deep breath as my reason for being at the Lufkin's came rushing back.

Whassup little sis?

At lunch w Sandy. Check out selfie!

A photo came through with Chili beaming and Sandy planting a kiss on her cheek. They were, amusingly, wearing identical sparkly lip gloss, and I couldn't help but notice the happiness on Chili's face. My shitty mood thawed. But I didn't stop packing my crap.

Cute. Say hi to San.

We having so much fun. I luv Sandy. He's like the girlfriend I've never really had. When u coming home?

Soon. Might be coming home earlier. Make sure house is clean or else.

U coming home early? Why?

Good question.

Job may be done. Will keep you posted.

The door to the cottage flew open, and I tucked my phone into my jeans pocket.

Clover took one step into the room and stopped short. "Wha...what are you doing?" she asked, looking from me to my duffel and back again.

I took a deep breath. "I don't think this arrangement is working out."

My phone buzzed again. I pulled it out to find another photo of Chili and Sandy, clowning around, and returned it to my pocket.

And I was reminded I was doing this gig not because of Clover, nor because of my own ego or happiness. I was doing this for twenty-five thousand dollars. I was doing this for her. And for my parents. Some discomfort on my part was par for the course. Hell, I'd been through worse. Anyone who'd prepped for the PAC-12 swim championships had been through worse.

I had a damn paycheck to earn.

But that wasn't the only reason I was there. I strode over to Clover and put a hand on either side of her face. She looked up at me, and I felt that connection that'd been forming between us stronger than ever. "Will, I—"

"I was being impulsive. I'm not going anywhere." I bent to kiss her forehead. "I'm fine," I said, throwing my duffel back on the bed.

She followed me. "Okay. Are you sure?"

"Yeah. I'm sure."

"Good, because if I got another flat, who would I call?" She smiled with her head tilted, and I remembered the second reason I was sticking around. Forgive me, Zenia, forgive my own damn self...but I was going to be greedy and enjoy every moment of Clover I could.

"Not Rob, that's for sure."

She was irresistibly fresh-faced after her spa treatments. Not a trace of makeup, just a nice, healthy flush to her cheeks. "Were you thinking of leaving, for real?"

I grabbed a seat on the overstuffed sofa and pulled her down next to me, draping an arm around her shoulders and propping my feet on the rustic coffee table. "Yeah. I overheard your mom, and I had a moment where I was like 'fuck this shit.'"

Clover chuckled. "Yeah...Mom's like that sometimes."

"But it's all good. I'm here for you."

I tried to catch her eye, but she picked at a piece of lint on the sofa.

"What about you?" I asked. "Are things okay for you? Is your family staying off your back?" I knew better, but I wanted to hear her take.

She nodded. "They're still on me. I mean, my mom's not very discreet." She looked up at me. "How much did you overhear?"

I shrugged, not wanting to let her know that Hart had sort of brought up the subject of his wife the night before. "It doesn't matter."

Her hand went to her mouth, and when I lifted her chin to face me, a tear trickled down her cheek.

"What's going on?" I asked.

She took my hand and rubbed it on her cheek. "You've been so great. So nice, and so tolerant of my family."

I smoothed her hair back and pulled her to me.

"You've made it easy. You are an amazing woman. And you smell damn good. Is that the oil they used during your massage? It's all woodsy smoky or something."

"Yeah," she said, blowing her nose and laughing. "It is."

She got up from the sofa and positioned herself right in front where I sat on the edge of it. She pulled my greased-stained T-shirt up and over my head before running her fingers over my tattoos, tracing the curves and designs, like she was memorizing them via touch and not just sight. Her touch electrified every cell in my body, and that familiar stirring was back in my pants. Christ, I wanted her and molded my hand to her lush breasts, kneading and pulling her nipples through the thin fabric of her shirt, knowing already how much she dug it.

Her head dropped back lightly, and she moaned in response to my touch. This was going to be different from our quiet session of the night before, when I woke and found her in the dark, wet and ready.

No, today had been a bitch with all its ups and downs, and it was time for us to forget all about it. I wasn't going to take my time, this time.

It just wasn't an option.

I slid off my jeans, my hard cock giving away my intentions. I yanked her shirt off, and pulled her skirt down, and she stood before me, gloriously naked, so feminine and yet strong and sure of herself and who she was. A revelation blasted through me.

I loved her.

Oh shit. Did I just say *love*?

Like. I meant *like*.

As she stood before me, I nudged her feet apart with mine so I could reach my fingers into the cleft of her soaking pussy, where her clit hung, erect, sensitive, and heavy. I ran my thumb over the sensitive ridge, and she grabbed my hair for purchase, shuddering so hard her legs wobbled. Seizing my opportunity to push her to her edge, I filled her tight pussy with two fingers, deep, hard, and fast as she remained standing, reaching around with my other hand to clasp her ass and hold her steady. Still she held on to me with a death grip, all the while grinding her hips to meet my thrusts. Her head hung limp and her moans grew, alerting anyone passing by the cottage to how freaking much we enjoyed each other.

I didn't care. Tell her family, tell the whole fucking world. It was beautiful. *She* was beautiful.

I let go of her ass to reach into my jeans for a condom. While an instinctual, beastly part of me wanted to feel her bare pussy with nothing between us, I was in control enough to know I couldn't do that…yet. When I'd sheathed myself, I positioned Clover's legs on either side of my hips. Notching my cock at her slick opening, I looked at her.

"Are you ready, baby? Are you ready for my cock?"

She whimpered, letting go of my hair to hold on to the back of the sofa as she adjusted her knees. "Yes. Yes, Will, give it to me."

I lowered her hips until I felt myself in her folds. A little further, and her pussy gripped me so tight I had to hold my breath to keep from shooting too fast. I kept one hand on her lower back, and reaching around to her tits, lifted the right one into my mouth. I pulled her nipple with a suction so strong her pussy tightened like a vise around my cock, and she began to buck. Her whimpers turned into moans, and she flung her head back and forth, her black hair flying all over, covering us both. "Fuck Will, fuck fuck fuck—"

"Are you coming, baby? Are you coming on my cock?" I asked through gritted teeth, pulling her deeper onto my erection.

Her pussy convulsed around my dick, and when she lowered her face to mine and our lips met, I felt an eruption begin in my balls. I growled like an animal, and my cum spurted for what felt like an eternity.

I lay back, exhausted, nuzzling her skin, when she put a hand on her clit and got off another time while I rested inside her.

To think I'd been about to leave.

"Are you ready to meet Rob's family?" Clover asked, handing me a cup of coffee she'd just made.

I propped the bed pillows behind me and watched her putter around the cottage, freshly showered with wet hair, barefoot, in her short terry robe. Every time she reached for something I got a little glimpse of her lush ass.

Down, boy.

"I don't know," I said, taking a swig from my steaming cup. "Are they like him?"

Of course they'd be like him. *Just* like him. I was an idiot for even asking.

She smiled. "I thought of not telling you. Letting you find out for yourself. Seeing how you handle it."

The playful lift of her eyebrow made me roll my eyes, and I put my free hand over my face, groaning. "Cripes. Does not sound promising."

"You've got that right," she said, her gaze holding mine.

"So. Lay it on me."

She dropped her robe to pull on another one of her hot bikinis, this one turquoise, and this time didn't bother with a bathing suit cover up.

My dick stirred, and I was glad I was still under the covers. I'd already tasted her, but the more we meshed physically, the more I wanted to explore all we could do together, pushing the line more and more.

She caught me staring and turned around, giving me a little hip shimmy that had my cock already at three-quarters full. "His family makes him look like Ghandi."

Another fun day at the office.

"Well, I suppose we could just keep low profiles. Mind our own business. Hope they don't notice us floating around in our own corner of the pool," I suggested. "Maybe sneak off to go play our own games?"

"Somehow, I am not sure that will work, but hey—let's give it the old college try."

As we headed out the door, Clover grabbed a bathing suit cover up.

"Damn. I thought you were gonna let it all hang out," I said, smacking her curvy behind. Seriously, this girl had just the right amount of ass.

"Are you kidding? And let those creeps check me out? Not a chance. Well, until we get in the pool, that is."

Sanders—I guessed it was him—had laid out a table set for both families, covered in a white tablecloth and what appeared to be very expensive china.

Did real people really bring china out to the pool? It seemed so stupid. Poolside was the realm of plastic plates, red Solo cups, and paper towels, not china, silver, and crystal. But whatever.

On the overflowing buffet table were mounds of poached salmon, roasted vegetables, and a variety of exotic-looking fruits. After introductions, I loaded up my plate and took a seat at the far end of the table where I hoped nobody would bother with Clover and me.

Nothing to see here, folks. Keep walking.

But we were not to be so lucky.

Rob's younger sister, Talia, was hot on my trail, carrying an empty plate. Looking all of seventeen, she was already a man-eater who probably worshipped the Kardashians. She grabbed the seat next to me, and as if that weren't close enough, scooted her chair over several inches in my direction.

I looked around desperately until I found Clover trapped in conversation with Rob's mother, unable to break free. I put my plate in the spot opposite me to save her a seat and leaned toward Talia's ear.

"Hey, Talia, would you keep an eye on my place here? That food there is Clover's, and now I'm getting my own."

She beamed, patting her hand on my chair. "Sure thing, Will."

Cripes.

I loaded another plate of fine china with salmon and vegetables and made my way back to the seat that Talia was guarding like a dog with a bone.

Clover took her seat across from me. Talia didn't even look her way.

"Thanks for the plate, Will. Everything looks amazing," Clover said with one eye on her young 'competition.'

I reached across the table and squeezed her hand. "You're welcome baby."

Talia either didn't notice or didn't care, however, and her hand settled *waaaay* too high on my thigh. Especially for jailbait.

"So, Will," Mr. Van Newsom bellowed from the other end of the table, "how do you spend your days? Are you another young master of the universe, like our Robert here is?"

Seriously? The only master that Rob was, was a master asshole.

"No, I am not. Still in school, in fact."

I discreetly but firmly pushed Talia's hand off my thigh.

"Well, finish that up, young man. Fortune waits for no one." He turned to Clover's dad. "Isn't that right, Hart?"

"Yes. Absolutely," Hart said without much enthusiasm.

"Tell us, Will, where are you at school?" He turned to hand his plate to his wife. "Honey, will you get me another serving of that incredible salmon?"

Mrs. Van Newsom dutifully hopped up from her seat and hustled over to the buffet table.

"I'm at UCLA," I said, adding just a little bit of pride as Hart, the USC supporter, raised his glass in silent toast.

"Oh. Is that right?" Van Newsom said, looking confused.

What, had he never heard of UCLA?

"My Robert here went to Stanford for his undergrad before enrolling at Columbia for his MBA. I went to Yale, myself. In fact, every man in the Van Newsom family has attended an Ivy League institution."

"Yes, they have," Mrs. Van Newsom said, setting a full plate before her husband. "Even a few of the women, too," she said, eyeing Talia. "I'm sure that tradition will continue."

Clover spoke up. "Will's senior project was opening a food truck with some of his classmates. It was wildly successful. And he was on a swim team scholarship."

I winked at her from across the table. I didn't give a shit what those people thought of me, but I was charmed at Clover's attempt to come to my defense.

But the Van Newsom family was not impressed.

"Well, I am sure once you graduate, you'll be able to make something happen," Mr. Van Newsom said. "In fact, I bet Robert and his friends can make some introductions for you. How 'bout that, everyone?"

Over my dead body.

"Oh, not sure, Dad," Rob said. "You know how the gang prefers to hire guys from the Ivies. People you can depend on."

"Rob!" Jessamyn cried, her face pure mortification.

"Gee, thanks, Rob, but don't worry. I seriously doubt Will needs help from you or any of your jerkoff friends," Clover blurted out.

Apparently Rob's insults were just a warm-up.

"Now, kids—" Clover's mom started.

But Rob cut her off. "You know, Clover, if you had any brains or ambition, you wouldn't be stuck with this guy from the freaking Valley."

Clover looked around the table as it fell silent, forks hanging in mid-air, mouths open all around. Slowly, she got to her feet, turning an enraged eye down the table at Rob.

"What did you just say, you fucking asshole?" she asked. "Because I know you didn't just sign your own—"

I reached across the table for her arm. While it wasn't part of the job description, I still didn't want Clover starting a brawl over something the limp-dick loser said. "Clover, let's just get out of here. Sometimes, value isn't measured by pedigree...or any other kind of degree."

I hustled around to her side of the table and put a firm arm around her, directing her back to our cottage. But not without some resistance.

But Rob let out a loud snort. "Gotta let your girl do your bidding, huh?"

That was a step too far. In a flash so fast nobody had time to react to Rob's disrespect or my anger, I was next to him, my hands wrapped tightly in the little weasel's LaCoste polo collar. I yanked him to his feet, his face going white with fear.

Inches from his face, I growled, my voice low and deadly, "Buddy, you have trouble knowing when to shut your big mouth, don't you?"

I lifted him a little higher, until the only way he could continue standing was on his toes, and I twisted my wrist, my knuckles digging into his throat. His face turned beet red from the limited oxygen, and his eyes looked panicked as he grabbed at my forearms, desperate to be freed.

What the hell did he expect? You don't go through life with a mouth like his without getting your ass handed to you once in a while.

Hart slowly got to his feet. "Okay, guys, let's calm down. I think it's time for a swim. What does everybody say to that?" He looked around hopefully, and because I had huge respect for the man, I let go of Rob, who fell over his chair and tumbled into his ass. His mother gasped and ran to his side. Because, of course.

"I'm sorry, Hart. I'm sorry, everyone. Please excuse my losing control," I said, addressing the entire table. "It was not gentlemanly," I added, glaring at Rob, whose mom was trying to pull him to his feet.

Mr. Van Newsom just sat there with his mouth open.

I turned to Clover, who also seemed to like the idea of not being forced out of the party. "Let's go for a swim, baby. The water looks amazing." She held her head up and sexily walked to the pool. Pulling her cover-up over her head, she adjusted her tiny bikini bottom and dove in. I dove in behind her.

Now the table was *really* silent.

CHAPTER 11

CLOVER

Whew knew a family luncheon could turn into such a shitshow?

Leaning back against the edge of the pool, I couldn't take my eyes off Will swimming laps. He glided through the water like he was born in it, without making a single sound or splash. His strokes were perfect.

Just like he was.

Christ, I knew I shouldn't be getting attached, but how could I not? How could any woman resist him? Smart, kind, sexy, and freaking hotter than hell. And he'd dropped out of school to take care of his sister. He was the whole shebang wrapped up in a sexy tattooed package.

"Hey," he said, popping out of the water right in front of me, his black hair slicked back like a stealthy, dangerous animal.

"Hey, there," I said. "How was the underwater?"

The rest of the party had left the table and were gathered in small groups around the pool, chatting, while staff cleaned up the barely eaten lunch. Family feuds will ruin appetites that way.

"Great, although I wished I had my goggles with me." He reached to smooth a strand of hair off my forehead. "I'm sorry about earlier. I shouldn't have reacted the way I did. It was wrong."

How could I even describe how gorgeous he was at that moment, with drops of water running over his tattoos and down his chest? I wanted to pat him dry and have my way with him. Or leave him wet. Hell, if I didn't have a crowd near the pool, I'd have let him untie my bikini bottoms and we'd get busy right there in the water.

Either way, I wanted him. What was that man doing to me?

And I hated that he felt the need to apologize to me. In any other world he would have been free to deck the shit out of someone like Rob. I didn't like what this situation was doing to him. I doubted he did, either.

"Hey, whaddya say we dry off and go for a walk?" I offered.

"Let's do it," he said, wet muscles bunching while he jumped out of the pool. He turned and, taking me by both hands, lifted me out in one graceful motion. We put on our flip-flops to walk the gravel path, and holding hands, I led him to some old stables on our property, my absolute favorite thing about my parents' home. They were long abandoned but perfect for playing in when my sister and I were kids. I hadn't visited them in a while and guessed they'd be more ramshackle than ever. But that was part of their charm.

"Wow, look at this place," Will said as he ducked below the doorframe, his eyes wide. "Did you guys keep horses here?"

"Nope. We did not. These were here long before my family took over the property. I don't think there have been horses here for a hundred years," I told him. "When Dad bought this place, a lot of it was pretty old. I remember even as a little kid, there was a lot of renovation going on all the time."

He ducked his head into one stall after the other. "This must have been amazing when you were a kid. So many possibilities."

I looked around, flooded by memories of simpler times. "At one point, my parents were considering tearing it down. It had gotten pretty rickety, and they didn't want anyone to get hurt. Mom was especially worried about rattlesnakes. But Jess and I begged and begged, and my dad had it shored up." I rested my hand on one of the walls, carved up with years' worth of initials of all the people who'd been through the place.

"Hey, you need to add your initials." I reached for an old jackknife we kept on a beam just above our heads. It was still there and still reasonably sharp. "Here you go."

It took him a little time to find a good spot, but by the

end he'd carved a large *WA*. "This way you'll never forget me."

Like that would *ever* happen.

I clutched his arms, warm from the sun and still damp from our swim. "C'mon. Let me show you my favorite stall. Jess and I used to spend the night there in the summers. We had tons of campouts, and when we got older we'd invite friends."

"Friends, huh?" Will said teasingly. "So is this where—"

"No...and no, I won't tell you where that happened, either," I laugh. "Actually...maybe you'd be my first?"

As we stepped into the stall, the floor still covered with old hay, the door at the other end of the building creaked open. Will and I froze in our tracks, and just as I started to call out to see who it was, Will put a hand on my arm and a finger to his lips.

"I think it's Rob and his dad," he whispered in my ear.

We moved into the shadows toward the back of the stall and listened.

"I tell ya, Robert. I don't know why you let a guy like that get the best of you. You should have decked him but good," Mr. Van Newsom said.

I looked at Will, and he rolled his eyes.

I heard a big sigh. "I know, I know. I just didn't want to embarrass Jessamyn any more than she already is with that sister of hers and the tattooed guy from the Valley. What a couple," Rob said. "Low-class trash, Dad. Just low-class trash."

I clenched my fists, ready to explode, but when I looked at Will, he was shaking his head, holding back laughter.

Needless to say, Jess was not, and never had been, embarrassed of anything having to do with me. But it was good to know what Rob and his family thought, although it hardly came as a surprise.

"You know, Dad, there's something fishy about that Will guy. It just doesn't add up. Why would Clover date someone from the Valley who's not even out of school yet? I mean, she could date someone like me, you know, who has money and family connections."

Okay, *that* was funny. Will and I both doubled over in silent laughter.

"I'm going to find out more, Dad. The Lufkins should know who is staying on their property."

"Great idea, son. They'd be crazy not to be curious about that character," Mr. Van Newsom said.

While their level of delusion was laughable, it also broke my heart that my sister was about to marry such a dirtbag. I had to do something. The question was, *what?*

"C'mon," Rob's dad said. "Let's get back to the party and that spread they call *lunch*. And for god's sake, why don't they fix up this barn? It's such a piece of shit. That Hart Lufkin, I just don't get him. Cheap bastard."

The barn door creaked open and then slammed shut behind them.

"Wow. Just wow." Those were the only words I could manage.

"Does your sister have any idea what she's in for?" Will asked.

How could she not know what a jerk that man was? I mean, it was as plain as the nose on his face. "I have to talk to Jess. Tell her everything," I said. "Even if she says she still wants to marry him, I need to know she's going in with her eyes open."

"Wait," Will said. "I have an idea. Let's fuck with them." A huge smile spread across his face.

"Yeah? How?" I asked.

"I don't know yet. But I have an idea."

I reached for the sides of his beautiful face, darkened by shadows. "You're so hot when you're being devious."

He dropped his head back and laughed. "Well, idiots like that are not too hard to outsmart."

I stood on my toes and planted a juicy one on his lips.

"Mmmm," he murmured. "So...you said first time?"

I stuck my head over the stall door to double-check that we were alone. Then, I slipped my fingers into the waistband of his swim trunks and ran them along the elastic that sat on his trim waist. "First time."

Looking down at me, he tilted his head and smiled.

I slowly lowered myself to my knees, taking his trunks with me until they reached his ankles, and he shook one foot out of them. He reached one hand to the wall just next to us and spread his feet apart.

From my perspective, down on my knees, he was a perfect specimen of humanity. His thigh muscles bulged, and his hard cock hung heavy between his legs. His trim waist opened to his broad chest and shoulders, and then there was his face. Chiseled, masculine, with just enough scruff for a hint of bad boy.

Player couldn't have sent me anyone better.

Ugh. Why did I let that thought enter my head? I was in a fantasy, and any thought of reality didn't belong. Instead, I had my man ready and willing, and I was going to worship him the way I wanted.

I cupped his balls with one hand and directed his cock toward my lips, rubbing his precum all over them and licking his sticky tang.

So good. And so goddamn hot.

"Baby likes my cum?" he murmured.

"Mmmm." It was all I could say. I'd wrapped my lips around his huge head to tease his tip with my tongue. Then I ventured further down his length. I'd wanted to take my time, but I just couldn't. I needed his cock in my mouth and down my throat.

God, I was becoming such a dirty girl.

And I loved it.

With one hand on his balls, I used the other to grip the root of his erection and pistoned over his length until he slammed the back of my throat, over and over. Tears streamed down my face as my gag reflex went wild and left me choking and sputtering. But I didn't care. Not one bit. I wanted him to face fuck me while I deep throated his cock, and show him that yes, I was his. His girl, his bitch, his slut…I didn't care. I was *his*.

His hands tangled in my hair, and while I could tell he

was trying not to hurt me, his control was shaky at best. It was so powerful, knowing I could drive this perfect man wild and make him lose control. As I lowered my mouth over his cock, he pushed his hips forward to go deeper. My hair flew around my face, and my bathing suit top hung off me, somehow having come untied behind my neck.

Will released a bellow that echoed through the empty stables, and he pounded the wall where he been holding himself up.

"Fuck, baby, take my cum, take it..."

His coming in my mouth was sexy enough, but when he piled his dirty talk on top of it, well that was just about all I could take. I swallowed every drop he gave me, and when he was done shaking, licked him completely clean.

"Jesus, Clover, that was un-fucking-believable..." He gripped my arms and pulled me to my feet. Planting a hard kiss on my mouth, he pulled me to him, cradling me tightly.

It seemed like he wanted to say something. I knew *I* did.

But we kept our thoughts to ourselves. It was for the better. At least for the time being.

"Shall we head back?" I asked, shaking out his straw-covered swim trunks.

"Let's do it. I think I can walk," he said laughing. He turned me around and tied my bikini top back up.

I adjusted the girls to make sure nothing was hanging out.

"Guess I wore you out?" I asked teasingly, watching him cover his beautiful cock back up with his trunks.

"Not even," he said with that damn hot smile.

Will and I stumbled back to our cottage, a little weary but very happy with our tryst in the stables. I had to admit that, growing up, I'd kissed more than one boy back there. But I'd never done what Will and I just had.

We walked with arms draped around each other, drunk with a lust we were only just beginning to understand the magnitude of. If I wasn't careful, I'd have a big problem on my hands.

But for now, I was going to enjoy the problem all that I could.

"Hey, Hart," Will called to my dad, who was watching us from the pool with a huge smile spread across his face.

Seemed I wasn't alone in my regard for our houseguest.

"Clover? Will? You guys up?" Jessamyn called from outside the cottage.

Seemed she was always catching us in bed. Whoops.

I sat straight up, still wearing my bikini. Will sprawled next to me in his trunks.

"Oh my god, I guess we dozed off," I said.

"C'mon, guys, get ready. We're going out on the boat," Jess said.

"Oh right. Dang, I forgot. We'll be there in ten, Jess."

Will leaned over me, and I flopped back onto the pillows. "Sure we have to go?" he asked with a devilish smile. "I still haven't done what I thought I'd want to do."

"I'd actually rather stay here and find out what that is, but family calls," I said. "Sorry. I promise, though…we'll get our chance later."

"I'm right behind you all the way, then," he said, picking me up by the waist and kissing me.

God, what was I going to do with this guy? And what if Rob had been serious about digging up dirt?

Things could get ugly, really fast.

Uglier than they already were.

CHAPTER 12

WILL

While Clover was busy making herself even more beautiful than she already was, I stepped outside the cottage to call Chili. And if I had a moment after that, I'd be making a call to Zenia. She needed to be made aware about Rob and his father poking around about me. There was something about my new 'friend' Rob that tickled my Spidey Senses…and if anyone could have helped me, it was Zenia. Maybe a 'counter' background check was in order.

First, though…Chili. "Hey, sis," I said when she answered.

"Hey, how's everything? You guarding lots of bodies?" she asked, shrieking with laughter. "Hopefully hot ones?"

I felt badly for lying. But what could I do?

"That I am, little sister. And yes, it's very, very hot."

"Are they paying you a lot, Will?" she asked.

If she only knew. Which she never would.

"They are. Otherwise, I wouldn't be doing it. You think I like staying away from you? It's so much more fun to watch your crazy antics up close and personal."

She harrumphed. "What antics?" she asked mock indignantly.

"You don't want to have this conversation, Chili," I said, laughing.

I didn't have the energy to go there, anyway. I was saving mine up for the shitshow that was sure to be dinner.

Trapped on a yacht. With a family of assholes.

"It's all good, big brother. Besides, Sandy's a total trip. He said when I turn eighteen, he's going to teach me all the secrets he knows to making a guy happy. He's like, not into me, but—"

"All right, all right. I don't need to think about you and guys. Not yet, anyway. We'll discuss that later."

"Okay," she answered. "Hey, a letter came from the courts. It says 'Guardian of Charlene Adams.' I guess that would be you, huh?"

"More or less, yeah. Would you please put that in my room with my other mail?"

Christ, it was probably another court date. We'd had so many I was practically on a first-name basis with the security guard. If we spent much more time there, I was certain they'd give me my own parking spot.

"Sure. And Will? I was invited to a sleepover. Can I go?"

I saw the Van Newsoms making their way toward the main house.

"I guess so. Text me the parents' name and phone number. I'll call them to check in. And and tell Sandy and Richard. They'll make sure it's all good."

"Oh thank you, thank you, Will. I swear, you can trust me now. No more trouble."

Chili might have been out of trouble, but that didn't mean I was.

I drove Clover and myself to the marina where her dad kept his boat. As she chattered on the way down the hill her parents' house was perched on, my mind wandered to how, on the boat, there would be no easy escape, should things get uglier than they had been over lunch. Once the boat left its slip, we were all stuck together in tight surroundings, like it or not.

The yacht was loaded with everyone but us.

"C'mon, kids!" Clover's mother waved.

Not surprisingly, once the cruise was underway, Talia was back at my side. The second Clover wasn't looking, she accidentally on purpose leaned against me, blaming it on the ocean swells.

Try again, honey. The sea was not that rough.

"Will, I wanted to tell you earlier today that I just love all your tattoos," she gushed. Her top was about two sizes too small, and I shivered inside, wondering if Chili was thinking like this girl. I hoped not, or else my little sister was going to end up in a nunnery.

"Thank you." I inched away from her to put some space between us.

"I was thinking of getting one myself," she said.

"That's nice."

"Actually, can you keep a secret, Will?" she asked.

I looked around for Clover, who was on the other end of the boat, with her arm around her sister. What was up with that?

"Will? Did you hear me?" Talia tugged on my arm.

"Yes, sorry. What were you saying?" I asked.

I needed rescuing, and I needed it fast.

"Well, I wanted to share a secret." She looked up, hoping for some comradeship.

"Okay. What?" I looked at Santa Barbara in the distance, getting smaller and smaller.

"I already have a tattoo," she whispered, looking around. "Don't tell my parents. They'll kill me. They think only sluts get tattoos."

Why was I not surprised to hear that? "I guess you'd better keep it hidden from them, then."

"I do. I really do. But I'll show it to you. It's right—" She pulled the neckline of her shirt open and began sliding her bra aside.

Uh-oh. I popped to my feet and made my way over to Clover.

She and Jess stopped talking the minute I arrived. But I didn't care if I were interrupting them. Having Rob's sister all over me was a disaster waiting to happen.

"Hey, ladies," I said. Jessamyn's eyes were red, and Clover's face was nothing but concern.

"Can I get either of you a drink?" I offered.

Clover nodded. "That would be great. White wine for us both."

As I wandered around looking for a waiter and wondering how the hell I would survive two hours in what was pretty much a floating prison, I stopped short in my tracks. I heard Rob's dad in conversation with Hart just around the corner, and I really didn't want to get caught up in it. I ducked around the corner and just listened.

"So, how big is this baby?" Mr. Van Newsom asked.

"She's forty foot," Hart answered. "I had her fully restored last year."

"Ah, very nice. I mean, if you've got to have a small yacht, this is the perfect size to have. And retro always has its niche."

With all that man had, he still had to compete? Over a stupid boat? It seemed to be a family weakness or something.

"Yup," Hart answered, and I could hear it in his voice… he didn't like the man, either.

"Say, I meant to ask you about the young man your daughter is with," Mr. Van Newsom said.

Hart cleared his throat. "You mean your son Rob? Who is about to marry my Jessamyn?"

Oh, *damn*. That was a good one.

"Um, no Hart. I think you know that's not who I meant."

Silence. I wished I could see, just so I could catch a glimpse of how Hart stared people down.

"I mean the man Clover is with."

I inched closer, straining my ears. I wanted to hear everything to know what I was up against. It could come in handy later.

"What about him?" Hart asked impatiently.

"Something about him doesn't seem quite right," Mr. Van Newsom.

"Not sure what you're getting at, but I'm not sure I want to know. Tom, let me be frank. I don't take well to gossips, much less malicious gossips. And I really do not care for people who think their family name and pedigree make them better than hardworking people trying to make their lives better. But I'm sure that's not what you are. Right?" Hart said.

"Well, Hart, you don't have to put it *that* way. I mean, c'mon. We're about to be family. We need to share information. Keep our families safe. Right?"

Hart was silent for a moment and then called out to anyone who could hear, "Hey, I think we're far enough out now to fish, everybody."

Their footsteps got closer before I could make myself scarce, and Hart ran right into me as he rounded the corner.

"Will!" he said, steadying himself by grabbing the rail. "Jesus, for someone as big as you are, you're damn near a ninja sometimes!"

"Oh hi, Hart. Just getting drinks for your two girls," I said as nonchalantly as I could.

"Okay, well, you're headed the wrong way. The waiter is over there," he said, pointing.

I looked in the distance and saw that, yes, the waiter was just a few feet away. And of course, it was Sanders.

"Excellent, Hart. Thanks."

"Hey, join us for some fishing, why don't you?" he asked. "The halibut's supposed to be great in the channel around here."

"Sure, that sounds great," I said. I'd always loved fishing. How bad could it be with the Van Newsom family? I mean, could they possibly screw that up like they had lunch?

I saw Jessamyn and Clover sunning themselves at the other end of the yacht. "Let me get drinks, and I'll be right back," I said. "Made a promise to the ladies."

I snagged two glasses of chardonnay and dropped them with Clover and her sister. "Hey, baby," I said to Clover, "you mind if I fish with the guys?"

She reached up to plant a kiss on my cheek. "Not at all. Have fun. Stay out of trouble." She winked dramatically.

I winked back to let her know that I planned to stay out of trouble at all costs. No need to add tension to an already difficult situation. That's when I realized no matter how many beautiful women there might be around—Clover was the one I had eyes for. I didn't care how corny that sounded.

I forced myself away from her and back to the stern where someone from the crew was setting up the fishing equipment. It revealed that Sanders had at least one weakness—apparently the man didn't know how to string a fishing pole.

"Hey, Will, you ever fish out here?" Rob asked as I saddled up and took an offered pole from a crewmember.

"No, Rob, I have not."

Hart stepped between the two of us, obviously wanting to prevent another incident, and reached his pole over the side of the yacht. "You're going to love it, Will. Best spot around, and this late in the day should be perfect for a great catch. And none of that chum cheating. We're going to do it the right way, spinners and jigs."

Not five minutes went by when there was a tug on Rob's line. A *hard* tug.

"Guys, check this out," he said, reeling in his line.

It took work, but Rob pulled in a huge one. I couldn't identify it, but it might have been great for the night's dinner.

"Get a picture of me, Dad," Rob called, struggling to hold the flopping fish.

"Got it, son," the beaming Mr. Van Newsom said as he stuck his iPhone back in his pocket.

"You got a good one there, Rob," Hart said. "But you have to throw it back in, you know."

Rob's face darkened. "Like hell I will. I worked for that fish, and he's mine now."

Hart shook his head slowly. "I'm serious, Rob. We can't keep it."

Rob rolled his eyes and looked to the horizon and then back to Hart. "You're kidding, right?"

Hart frowned. "I am not. That's a giant sea bass. It's red flagged here in Cali. Here, let me help you cut it loose."

Rob jerked the fish out of Hart's reach. "Sorry. No."

When he pulled the fish out of Hart's reach, he'd moved it in my direction. In one swift movement, I grabbed a knife out of the tackle box, cut the line, and threw the fish back in the Pacific.

"What the fuck?" Rob screamed.

Alerted, Clover and Jessamyn started making their way to our end of the boat.

"You heard the man," I said, quietly. "You don't risk a man's fishing license or a fine from Fish and Game because you want a trophy."

Rob looked like he wanted to hit me, but common sense must have overtaken him, because he held back. He gave me an icy glare and then laughed.

"Sensitive, are you, Will? Well, throw the goddamn fish back in. I didn't want it anyway," he said.

Jessamyn, just arriving, put her arm on Rob's. "Rob, please—"

He shook her off and started to walk away.

Jessamyn stood there red-faced, and her father looked down, shaking his head.

"Rob," I said, "some men don't have to prove themselves by taking something they're not entitled to."

He stopped and turned, staring me down. If looks could

have killed, I'd be a goner. But fortunately, they don't. Fortunately for Rob, that was. Because I would have happily tossed his ass into the Pacific if he'd tried to start anything.

"Go fuck yourself, Will," Rob snarled, disappearing with Jessamyn just behind him.

But Clover beamed. That's my girl.

Hart cleared his throat and spoke up. "Shall we cast again, my friends? See if we can catch something we're allowed to keep?"

I had a feeling that the big fish wasn't the only thing Rob might not end up keeping.

CHAPTER 13

CLOVER

Fortunately, my dad's boat was big enough that my sister and I were able to find a quiet spot to catch a few late-afternoon rays and gab.

"That sister-in-law-to-be of yours is a piece of work," I said.

Jess frowned. "Talia? I don't know what you mean."

I sat up on my beach towel. "Are you serious? You haven't seen her throwing herself at Will? I'm embarrassed for her. What a little fool. An underage one at that."

"Oh, that. Yeah, she does that." Jess pursed her lips. "She's a mess, and her parents are in complete denial. Trust me, that chick's going to end up making headlines on TMZ someday if she has her way."

I gawked at my sister. Did she really want to marry into that horrible family?

"Hey, Jess, are you sure about all this? You know, the wedding and stuff?" I asked.

I braced myself. My sister wasn't prone to explosions, but my question would surely hit a sore spot.

And I was right as she bolted upright. "What the hell are you saying—"

I put a finger to my lips. "Wait. Shhh." I lowered my voice to a whisper. "I can hear Mrs. Van Newsom and Mom talking about us."

They clearly didn't know we were within earshot.

"You know, Patsy, I don't understand why your daughters wear those skimpy bikinis. They've both landed nice men," Mrs. Van Newsom said. "Just because you've got it doesn't mean you should... flaunt it like a heifer for sale at an auction."

Jess and I looked at each other, sharing expressions of shock.

"Oh my god," Jess whispered, her eyes bugging. "Did that bitch just call us heifers?"

I nodded and kept listening. I'd have to thank Mrs. Van Newsom later for helping make my point.

"I think the girls look just fine in their bathing suits. They're young and have beautiful figures," my mom said calmly. "If I were still that trim, I'd be out there in a bikini as well."

Big sigh on the part of Mrs. Van Newsom. "Okay. Then take a look at my Talia. *She* doesn't dress like that. She's still trying to attract a man but dresses like a *lady*."

Jess leaned close to my ear. "Her darling Talia would go

down on the entire Lakers starting lineup if she had the opportunity to get famous as an Instagram influencer or for some coke."

I snapped my head in Jess's direction and whispered back to her. "No way. How do you know she does coke?"

Jess rolled her eyes. "Get her alone, overlook the wine she'll guzzle like it's orange juice, and let the slut talk. She makes Paris Hilton look like Pollyanna."

"Her mother is seriously delusional. Wow. Just wow," I said.

"Yeah, and if she doesn't shut up, Mom might throw her overboard," Jess said.

At the thought of that, I started shaking with quiet laughter, the "church giggles," as Jess had always called them. Hysterical laughter takes over at the very moment you shouldn't be laughing at all. Jess took one look at me and started laughing, too.

"I can see Mom throwing her overboard," she said, gasping for air.

In my effort to remain silent, I accidentally snorted, which of course led us into another round of giggles.

"C'mon," I said. "Let's go to the back where the guys are fishing. We gotta get away from the 'moms'."

What was it about laughing when you weren't supposed to that made things a thousand times funnier than they really were?

But things in the back of the boat weren't exactly funny. It seemed the men were in a pissing match about whether they could keep or throw back a huge fish hanging from the line in Rob's hand. After some testy words, Will cut the bruiser loose, and it swam off in the Pacific Ocean.

Jess was mortified, and even more so when Rob rebuffed her efforts to support him.

But Will was my new freaking hero. He'd done the right thing from what I could hear. Nothing was more delicious than seeing a douchebag like that eat humble pie.

While my sister took off running after her asshole, I couldn't take my eyes off Will. If there hadn't been so many people around, I wouldn't have been able to take my hands off him, either.

He looked over, gave me a slow look from head to toe and a nice, sexy wink, and turned back to his fishing.

Holy shit. I immediately started plotting when I could next get him alone.

"Hey, honey," my dad called, distracting me from my hormones and primal instincts. "You want to join us? The fish seem to be biting."

Why not? Jess was chasing after her idiot fiancé, Mrs. Van Newsom was trashing my sister and me to my mom, and Talia was god knew where but most likely snorting white stuff up her nose. What a group.

"Sure, Dad. Hook me up."

It seemed that Rob had caught the last fish that was willing to bite, because no more fish joined our party. But I was next to Will, literally with my head on his shoulder, as we watched Santa Barbara rise out of the sea in the distance. Its mountains climbed high, and small illuminations twinkled here and there as the sun went down and people switched on their lights. In the other direction, facing west, the sun slowly lowered over the Pacific Ocean, which stretched into infinity.

My happiness was momentarily invaded with a sad thought, that my sister had brought someone like Rob into our family. But I knew from experience that people had to make their own decisions. I sure was glad I'd made the one I had that weekend, even if it was only a temporary arrangement.

Speaking of temporary arrangements, I needed to find out how this sort of thing worked for Player. What if I wanted to see Will again—which, to be honest, I was pretty damn sure I would want. Was that out of the question, unless I wanted to 'hire' him?

But I pushed practical thoughts like that out of my head. I had a bit of time left with Will, and I planned to make the most of it, even if I was dreaming of waking up next to him every day, and not just during my sister's wedding weekend. He really was the kind of guy I'd always hoped I'd end up with. Good-looking, smart, thoughtful, and alpha as hell, as evidenced by his takedown of Rob.

And I had a feeling we'd not yet seen the end of their run-ins. I could see a future of many family gatherings that consisted of Rob getting his ass handed to him by Will. It made the 'immature me' giggle violently.

As if he could read my thoughts, Will turned from

watching his fishing line and gazed directly at me, catching me off guard. "Hi," he said quietly enough so only I could hear. "You're beautiful."

I couldn't say a thing, only smile at him like an idiot.

And then, wouldn't you know, he planted the softest kiss on my temple.

Good thing I was leaning on the boat's railing, because I otherwise would have fainted dead away.

WILL

With Clover off soothing her sister after a somewhat disastrous cruise on her father's yacht, I showered and then went through my hanging bag to check out the duds Zenia had set up for me. Apparently fancy weddings like the one Jessamyn was having required all levels of formality, and I was to wear a tuxedo.

I hadn't worn one since my high school prom, not that I'd made that known to the group out on the boat earlier. That fucker Rob had a serious bug up his ass about me, and out of respect for Clover, I couldn't give him any more ammo than he already had for screwing things up with his lousy temperament.

When I pulled open the closet, I saw on Clover's side a collection of more high heels than I could even count. Who knew the down-to-earth schoolteacher had so much rich-girl crap? I didn't know the exact price tag, but I was certain just one pair of those skyscrapers was worth more than the entire wardrobe my mother had owned when she was still alive.

Just as I picked up one, wondering how my Clover could be so comfortable in two such different worlds, my phone rang.

It was Sean from Player. "Hello, my friend," I said.

I couldn't stop looking at all those stupid shoes.

"Hey, Zenia let me know you're needing a background check on someone. How can I help?" he asked. As the second-in-command there, he seemed to handle the—shall we say—*darker* side of the business.

I flipped the lock on the cottage door. If Clover were returning to our room, I wanted to make sure I had time to end the call.

"Sean, I appreciate your getting back. Hey, there's a character here named Robert Van Newsom. He's causing some trouble, and I wanted to know if you could check him out. You know, arrest records, school records—whatever you guys have access to."

"What level?" Sean asks. "There's easy, cheap, and free… and there's deep."

"Easy, cheap, and free, man. I don't think he's some deep-cover Russian spy or anything." I found myself pacing the room, so forced myself to take a seat on the sofa. The one where I'd been naked with Clover just a few hours before, and I could swear I could still smell her sweetness.

I heard Sean tapping on a computer keyboard. "Okay. I got it started. I'll send you anything I get right away."

"Thanks, man. I owe you. And Zenia, of course."

"Happy to help."

Speaking of Zenia, I realized I should have gone through the clothes she had pulled together for me earlier. In the hanging bag she'd filled for me, I found a bow tie. And not the kind that just snapped on.

Shit. I had no idea how to tie a bow tie. But how hard could it be?

I cleared my shower steam off the bathroom mirror, and with a towel around my waist, pulled the tie around the back of my neck. I proceeded to make a bow like the kind you make when you tie your shoe. And boy, did that look like dogshit.

Christ, what was I going to do?

I carefully untied my mess, knowing better than to yank on the delicate silk and destroy it altogether. Even though that's what I would have liked to do.

YouTube, don't fail me now. Time to help a player out.

Saved. There were more *how to tie a bow tie* videos than there were probably bow ties in the world. I clicked on one of a dapper-looking gentleman with a menswear channel. What did the world do before YouTube?

Charles, my new YouTube friend, walked me through every step. First, let the left side hang down two inches longer than the right. Tie a simple knot against the shirt's top button, and throw the long side back over the shoulder. Next, take the piece hanging down and wrap the widest part around your left finger and hold in front of top shirt button as a sort of half bow. Then, pull fabric that had been thrown over shoulder to the front, and let that hang down the middle of the chest…etcetera, etcetera, etcetera.

Holy shit. It was *almost* acceptable.

I untied my nearly-there tie and tried again. About five times.

And wouldn't you know, after several tries, it looked fucking awesome.

Not to mention hilarious, since I was standing there wearing nothing but a towel and the damn bow tie.

All right. Got that shit covered.

As I put my tux back into the closet, Clover's massive shoe collection caught my eye again. She sure did a good job of hiding her wealth. I doubted any of those fancy designer shoes were in the graduate-housing apartment she shared with her other student teacher roommate.

The worlds she and I came from were even more different than she could know. Sure, she might be studying to be a student teacher, but she'd never have to worry about paying a bill in her life. Shit, when she graduated, her dad would probably set her up in one of the fancy loft condos in downtown L.A. that were so popular.

But that was all right, because the woman rocked. She knew I was on my path, and she had massive respect for that. I wished I could introduce my sister to Clover and show her the Lufkin's property.

On the other hand, what would she think of the wealth I was currently surrounded by? I mean, hell *I* wasn't sure what to make of it. Talk about fucked-up values. Hart was cool, and Jess was okay beyond her horrible taste in men, but I was dubious about Patsy, and the Van Newsom family was a total mess. The worst of it was that they had no freaking idea how rotten they were.

Maybe that was why Clover hid her background from the real world. She'd seen close up and personal what massive wealth could do to people. As long as she could stay as far away from it as possible, she could pretend to be normal.

But I chafed that she had to hide her real self. Did she think regular non-rich people couldn't deal with her sort of privilege?

It all bummed me out a little because she was exactly the kind of woman I wouldn't mind dating. Smart, beautiful, sweet, sexy. Worth dealing with assholes like Rob that were part of her world.

Not that that was an option, anyway. I was being paid to be there, not find a new girlfriend.

I dressed in silk trousers and a linen shirt for the rehearsal dinner and went to Hart's library for a scotch to wait for the rest of the party. He joined me and we toasted his daughter. He was a good guy, and I'd miss him when my gig was over.

He reminded me a lot of my own dad—levelheaded, kind, hardworking.

He did his best for his family.

Finally, everyone was gathered in the room. Everyone, that was, but Clover.

I stood up, setting my scotch down. "Let me go find Clover. She was almost ready when I left her in the cottage."

But as soon as I'd finished speaking, she ran into the room. "Oh my gosh, I'm so sorry, everyone. I didn't mean to be late," she gushed, pushing a couple of wild strands of black hair out of her face.

It was all I could do to keep from taking her back out of that room and to our cottage so I could have my way with her. She was so beautiful, her lightly tanned skin glowing, her eyes sparkling. She was wild and free, sexy and saucy and seductive.

But that would have to wait until later.

"It's no problem, darling," Patsy said. "Everyone just arrived. And don't you look lovely?"

And boy, did she ever. Her black hair hung loose and wavy, a real contrast to the tightly pulled hairstyle her sister was wearing.

And then there was her dress, a gauzy, darkish blue strapless number that reached to the floor, puddling around her little silver sandals. It perfectly highlighted her curves, making my mouth water as my tongue wanted to trace every inch of what the dress covered, just to double check she was as delicious as she'd been before.

She was a vision. That's all there was to it. I had no idea how I'd make it through the dinner without ravishing her.

So I started by taking her hand.

The same small bus that had ferried everyone to the marina earlier was waiting in front of the Lufkin's home. We climbed back in and made our way to the country club for the dinner that I was told was would be intimate but actually consisted of about a hundred guests.

That's what people called *intimate*?

As we rode over, I noticed Clover looking out the bus window, and while I couldn't be certain, it seemed like she was avoiding my gaze. I figured she was nervous about the event and needed to gather her thoughts. So I leaned over the aisle and shot the breeze with her mom. The woman might not have thought I was right for her daughter, but she was nice on the surface and was warming to me. I guess that's what mattered most with these people.

How things looked on the surface.

We walked into a vast rehearsal dinner, full of a glamorous group of powerful and rich men and women, and I was reminded of why Zenia'd picked me for this. I was gloriously anonymous to this roomful of potential Agency clients. Thankfully. The room was fragranced by exploding flower arrangements and dimly lit by candles and paper lanterns hung from the ceiling. A quartet played off in the corner, and the buzz of conversation and clank of expensive silverware and crystal turned up the energy in the room. In spite of myself, I realized I had a smile on my face as I took a seat next to my beautiful Clover—

Shit, did I just say *my*? God, I was in deep shit, and I didn't care.

—and placed a hand on her thigh. I lowered my voice. "Is everything okay?" I asked, taking a deep breath, savoring her perfume.

She clutched my fingers and looked up at me with a small smile. "Yeah. Everything's great."

I couldn't know for sure, but I suspected maybe she was thinking like I was.

That after the wedding tomorrow, our little romance would be over. Forever.

But I had a few more hours with her, and I was going to make the most of them. I waved over the server for some of the wine we'd tasted at the Owenses' vineyard.

I spotted the Van Newsoms on the other side of the room, holding court with their invitees, and Rob and Jessamyn greeting guests as the door. Jessamyn pointed some weird-looking dude in our direction, but when he got a look at me sitting with Clover, scowled and skulked away.

I nudged Clover. "Hey, is that guy The Jester? The one you told me about?"

She craned her neck and nodded. "Yup. The one and only. Is he coming over here?"

"Nah. When he saw me, he boogied in the opposite direction."

Clover laughed, and we clinked our wine glasses, both feeling pretty much like we'd won the lottery.

After a killer dinner of filet mignon, Hart stood at a microphone and held his glass up to the room, which slowly quieted down. Seemed it wasn't easy to corral one hundred guests who were enjoying their food and wine.

Rob's best man spoke first and said something marginally intelligent. Nothing unexpected there. Then, Clover stood and talked about her sister, and her family, and the Van Newsoms, who were now their new family. Her parents beamed.

Clover might have been smiling brilliantly, but I knew she was choking on those words.

Finally, the happy couple stood at the mic, and the room went dead quiet as Jess thanked everyone for coming. Rob started blathering, his speech thick from too much wine, with some bullshit talk about now having two excellent dads, and two excellent moms, and two sisters with the addition of the beautiful Clover. He pointed her out, and everyone clapped politely.

She continued to smile but gripped my fingers.

When he finished, we turned back to our tablemates, ready for the next part of the evening.

But, as it turned out, Rob was not done.

"And one more thing about my smokin' hot sister in law—"

The smile could not have fallen off Clover's face faster. I glanced over at Jessamyn, and her mouth hung open.

Everyone in the room looked up.

"Did you all notice that during her speech to my future wife and myself, she didn't mention her man? That guy sitting over there." He pointed at me and smirked.

What was he up to? Things were not going to end well

for that asshole if he didn't sit down and shut his goddamn mouth.

"Yup, she didn't say a word about him. You want to know why?" He scanned the room gleefully.

Just then Jessamyn reached for the mic. But Rob pushed her away, causing her to stumble back. She caught on the edge of her chair, shrieked, and went over, hard. Hart jumped up to help. And Rob did nothing.

A gasp went through the crowd while he continued, uninterested in the fact that his fiancé was sprawled on the floor behind him.

"Well, I want to let you all know I've learned something very interesting about the type of family I'm marrying into. My big sis here, Clover, has *hired* this guy to be her date this weekend. Yes, I have discovered she hired—wait for it —a *male escort*. Classy lady, huh? Ladies and gentlemen, meet Clover's *fake date*."

"Oh my god," Clover whispered.

"*That's enough! Shut your mouth, you little—*" Hart bellowed as he dashed toward Rob while Patsy tended to a sobbing Jessamyn.

But I was faster. Of course I was faster. I had thirty years on the man. I couldn't hear anything. Couldn't really see anything, either. Except for Rob's evil fucking grin.

And my fist smashing into his face.

CHAPTER 15

CLOVER

I wasn't surprised to find, when I pushed up my eye mask, that the sun was blazing through my cottage's shutters.

The cottage I'd shared with Will.

I also wasn't surprised to find my head throbbing with a polite reminder that I'd finished the entire red bottle of wine on the floor next to my bed. Clothes were strewn all over the room, and there was a broken wine glass in the corner. Will's side of the closet was empty, my mouth was dry, and my stomach was churning.

Basically, I wanted to die. And not just because I felt like total shit.

The horror of the nightmare that had been my sister's rehearsal dinner came flooding back, not that it had been that far from my thoughts, but blessed sleep had let me pretend for a few tossing and turning hours that maybe my life was not a grade A mess.

But it really *was* a grade A mess.

I pushed myself to the side of the bed, and the entire room moved. Squeezing my eyes tightly closed helped. But I couldn't keep my eyes closed all damn day.

Or could I?

I flopped back on my bed and opened one eye just enough to see if my phone was within reach. I had to know what time it was. If it was late enough, the chances were good I'd missed my sister's wedding. Sounded terrible, I know, but it was the last place on earth I was going to show my face.

How did I end up in such a shitty situation? Hiding who I really was?

I had to hide my family background.

I had to hide that I was happily single.

And worst of all, I'd had to hide the feelings I had for Will.

How had life taken such a turn for the worse? Only a couple weeks ago I'd been moving through my master's degree program, rocking my student teacher gig, and feeling generally pretty good about life. But then my sister's wedding drew near, and I made some bad decisions out of shame and desperation.

But not anymore. No, I was done second-guessing myself. And I was going to stop giving a shit about what other people thought of me.

I forced myself to sit up in bed and keep my eyes open.

The room spun for a minute or two, so I took deep breaths to ward off the menacing nausea. Sheer will allowed me to get my feet under myself, and I grabbed some jeans and a T-shirt out of a dresser, and pulled on my Converse high tops. Moving as quickly as my poor head would let me, I shoved all I could into my suitcase and placed the empty wine bottle and shards of the glass I must have dropped at some point into the trash. I collected my toiletries, and in one last look around to ensure I hadn't missed anything, I checked the hook on the back of the bathroom door.

That's when my new-found commitment fell to pieces. I'd congratulated myself way too early.

Damn if there wasn't, right in front of my face hanging on the back of the bathroom door, one of Will's rock 'n' roll T-shirts. It stared back at me, mocking my new resolve.

I reached for the soft worn cotton as if I were touching him. Something I'd never get to do again.

I pulled it up to my face and inhaled his spicy, clean scent. Something else I'd never get to do again.

And the tears came.

With his T-shirt in my hand, I fell to my knees on the hard bathroom tile and dropped my head to the floor while my body convulsed with sobs. It was as if a lifetime of sorrows had decided to invite themselves to the party that was my life. Given the choice, I would rather they have stayed in the background where they had existed for so long. But it seemed like what I wanted didn't matter.

Will was gone.

I used his shirt to catch my tears, and the night before played out in my memory like I was watching a movie.

Rob Van Newsom, the horrible, horrible man my sister must, by that time of the day, have gotten married to, had outed Will in the cruelest, most sadistic way imaginable. The pleasure he took in humiliating my entire family and me was beyond sickening. And I had to suffer through his presence for the rest of my life because he had made himself part of my family.

My heart broke not only for my sister, but also my parents, who deserved to see their daughter with a decent man, and who I knew would probably end up suffering even more than the rest of us. Watching their daughter go through life with a man who pushed her to the ground the night before their wedding, in front of a crowd of one hundred of their closest friends and family, was a massively heartbreaking proposition.

After Will had slugged Rob and knocked him out cold, pandemonium broke out. Mr. Van Newsom started screaming for the police while his wife cried for an ambulance for her precious son. Will had turned to my father and apologized for any trouble he'd caused the family and then turned to me. I was by that time right next to him.

He was leaving. "I'm sorry, Clover, but things didn't work out. I'm going back to the cottage to pack my bag. I'm getting the hell out of here. I don't want to cause you any more trouble."

I just stood there, mutely nodding, looking at the

broken-hearted faces of my parents. I helped my sobbing sister to her feet, and shortly thereafter, all the guests made for the door in a slow and silent fashion. It was like a funeral.

I guess something *had* died, truth be told.

I pulled myself off the bathroom floor, stuffed Will's shirt into my purse, and texted my roommate, Sarah, that I was on my way back to our apartment. Just as I took one last look around the cottage—hoping I wouldn't find anything else of Will's—there was a knock at my door.

Odd. Jess's wedding reception should have been in full swing at the country club—that was, if any of the trauma-tized guests had returned for more of my family freakshow.

I peeked out the window, and who was standing at the door but my sister. In her custom lace wedding dress and veil, no less.

What the hell?

"Jess?" I asked, pulling the door open. All I could do was stare at her. For a bride on her wedding day, she looked less than happy.

She sighed. "Can I come in?"

"Oh, yeah, of course. Sorry, I was just so shocked to see you here," I said. "You look amazing."

She plopped down on the edge of my bed. "Thanks. I've never felt prettier." She shrugged and laughed lightly, picking at the mud and dirt on the bottom of her dress. Where the hell had she been dancing?

I took a seat next to her. "I'm so sorry, Jess. About everything. For ruining your day, for lying to you—especially for lying to you."

She looked down at her hands, which were folded in her lap.

And don't you know it, my tears returned. "Jess, I did hire Will, to get Mom and everyone off my back. But in the end I liked him. I really did. And now I'll never see him again."

She shook her head slowly. "You didn't ruin my day. You actually *made* my day."

"Huh?"

"If it wasn't for you, I'd be married to that asshole right now." She turned to look directly at me.

"Um. But you *are* married. Aren't you?" I asked.

"Nope," Jessamyn said, her face breaking out in a smile. "No, I am not."

"Okay, Jess. Is there something going on that I don't know?"

"Yeah. I didn't get married. Stood the loser up at the altar. I woke up, got all fixed up on auto-pilot, and then I came to my senses."

"*Get the fuck out*," I screamed, jumping to my feet. "You didn't!"

She broke into a huge smile and nodded with enthusiasm. "I didn't even go to the church. Only Mom and Dad know where I am. I was hiding in the stables all day."

"Is that why you smell kinda funny?" I asked, sitting back down. "And are so dirty?" I hadn't noticed before, but there was piece of hay sticking out of her perfectly coiffed hair.

She laughed and lifted her dress just enough to show off her white silk shoes. They were covered in both mud and hay.

My heart soared with happiness, and I threw my arms around my sister.

"Oh my god, oh my god. I'm so happy for you," I cried.

We held hands as tears streamed down both our faces.

She stepped back and spoke to me in a very serious tone. "You have to call him, Clover. You have to call Will. Get in touch with him, and you tell him what I've seen in your eyes for the past few days—the thing that I didn't have with Rob, and that I never would. You tell him he's a great guy and you can't let him slip through your fingers."

"I can't, Jess. I can't. I have no way to reach him except through Player, and they won't put us in touch unless it's for, you know, a *date*." I shook my head. Looked like both my sister and I were single once more.

"Well, I have a thought," Jess said. "Rob's family was able to dig up dirt on him by spending a bunch of money. We can do the same thing to track him down and find him. Hell, if anything, go down to the...Player? I've heard that name before. If you need to, hire him again, and greet him with your arms around his neck and your heart on your sleeve."

I thought of his T-shirt in my purse and my heart broke

a little more. "I'm sure he wants nothing to do with me. Or any of us. He's probably disgusted with us all. I texted my roommate I was on my way back."

"No, please don't leave yet. I need your help dealing with Mom and Dad and any other fallout that's sure to drop on my head."

"I don't know, Jess. I mean, I hate to leave you, but I really do need to get back to my classes and stuff," I said.

But she looked so despondent. "Please, Clover. Just for a few more days."

She was right. School was one thing, but as I'd always told my students, family comes first. "Okay. Okay. We'll face Mom and Dad together."

Jess threw her arms around me. "Oh thank you. Thank you. Now, I'd love to get this stupid dress and shoes off. Hiding in the stables all day was not my idea of fun. But I did see where Will carved his initials."

"Oh yeah. I forgot about that. I'd suggested he do it."

"Did you see what he carved?" she asked.

"Yeah. His initials, *WA*."

"Well he must have gone back and carved more," she said.

I wrinkled up my nose. "What do you mean?"

"There's a heart under the *WA*, and just under it are your initials, *CL*."

Oh.

I threw myself back on the bed. "What am I going to do?"

"C'mon. Get up. You're gonna help me out of this dress,

we're going to go out shopping and drop a shitload of money—Grade A retail therapy—and we're going to devise a plan to find Will."

The cottage my sister had shared with the jilted Rob was pretty much ransacked. The good news was that all his shit was gone.

"Guess I had a little visitor," she said, toeing something out of the way.

I looked around at the mess. "Looks like he packed his bags and got the hell out." I started picking up my sister's things, which the asshole had apparently felt free to throw all over, like a little kid having a temper tantrum.

"I'm sorry, Jess. Sorry about all of this."

"Clover, stop that. I'm not sorry. Not sorry at all. In fact, you know what?" she asked.

"What?"

"I think this is the best day of my life. And I have you to thank for it. You showed me that regardless of the plans, of Mom's pressure, of anything...I was about to marry an insecure flaming asshole. And that's no recipe for happiness."

I was startled by a mini-rush of joy. At least I'd done something right.

CHAPTER 16

WILL

I said goodbye to the shithole motel I'd just spent the night in, threw my stuff in the back of my Jeep, and said goodbye to Santa Barbara.

Hopefully, forever.

Seriously.

As good as it had felt to slug that asshole Rob for insulting Clover and her whole family—not to mention Jessamyn, the woman he was supposed to marry the next day—I knew I shouldn't have done it. If Zenia was willing to keep me on at Player—and that was a big *if*—I doubt I'd be getting paid for the job. Five days down the drain. Five days away from Chili, who needed me more than anything. She'd never been that big of a troublemaker, normal stupid teenage bullshit for the most part, but with our parents gone, she was vulnerable. And that scared the shit out of me.

I knew my parents, and if there was one thing in the world they'd ask of me, it would be to look after Chili. *Keep her on the straight and narrow*, as my dad would have said, and *make the family proud* as my mom would have.

Not sure I was managing either one very well at that moment. If Chili ended up in foster care, I didn't know how I would live with myself. She'd be off with some family that didn't know her, most likely in a strange town and a strange school, feeling the loss of our parents more intensely than ever.

And what would I do? Go back to school like nothing happened? Re-join the swim team? Get back to kickin' chicken with my buddies on the food truck?

I hadn't really cared that the douchebag Rob had tried to insult me. I couldn't give a shit about him, or his family. But when he tried to drag Clover through the gutter with his vicious words, well, that was more than I could take. I'd made my apologies, grabbed my stuff, and driven straight to a motel on the edge of Santa Barbara. I'd had a couple drinks and wasn't about to attempt the two-hour drive home.

Why was it that a kid like Chili got so ripped off—lost her parents just when she was on the cusp of becoming an adult—when pricks like Rob have everything and take it all for granted? In what universe is that fair?

And how could he weasel his way into a decent family like Clover's? Her sister, marrying that creep, needed to take a look at life and realize everything was not as it seemed.

So I was glad for the two-hour ride ahead of me. I needed to clear my head and come up with my next plan of attack.

"Chili," I said as soon as she'd answered the phone.

Big sigh. Seemed that was the hallmark of teenage-hood. "Will," she whined. "Why do you keep checking up on me?"

Um, because you recently stole a car and got arrested?

But I was not out to shame her. "I just wanted to hear your voice, sis." It was true.

"Oh. Okay. Well, I'm fine here. How's Santa Barbara? How do you like being a bodyguard?" she asked.

If she only knew...

"It's been fine, but I'm on my way home now."

"Really?" she asked, her voice perking up. "Can we go for tacos tonight? To that place Mom really liked?"

We were both silent for a moment when we realized Chili had referred to our mother in the past tense. There'd be a lot more of that going forward. Milestones, and all.

"We'll try. I'll see you soon, sis. I gotta run a couple errands before I get home."

"Sounds good. And I can't wait for tacos!"

Having made sure all was calm on the home front, my next order of business was to salvage my position with Player.

And to stop thinking about the lovely Clover. Shit, I wanted to call her. But I would work on that later.

I had to bring Zenia up to date on all that had happened before she found out from someone else. The last thing a woman like her wanted was to be blindsided by anything, much less information about one of her employees slugging someone during an engagement. I also needed to know what Sean might have found in the background check of Rob, not that it really mattered any longer.

As I neared L.A., I steered the car toward Melrose Avenue and Player. Not only did I need to have a face-to-face with Zenia, I needed to return the clothes.

When I arrived, I pulled into the first parking spot I found and grabbed the hanging bag from my trunk. When I'd left Santa Barbara that morning, I'd thankfully had the presence of mind to dress on the nice side, in trousers and a collared shirt. Not that I could have worn my favorite ratty T-shirt, anyway. Seemed I'd lost the damn thing.

I rang doorbell and was buzzed right in, but when I stepped inside the front door, I came face-to-face with Sean. Perfect timing.

I threw the hanging bag over my other arm so I could shake. "Hey. Great to see you."

"You too," he said. "Aren't you back early?"

"Um. Yeah. That's what I here to talk to Zenia about."

"Uh-oh. Was there trouble with that guy?"

I nodded. "Yup. Hey, did you get anything on him?"

"I did. Let me email the report to you. But in a nutshell, he was pretty clean, except for one thing."

"Yeah?" I asked.

"He was kicked out of Stanford for cheating on a Spanish test. He never graduated," Sean said.

"Well. I'll be damned."

No wonder the punk was so insecure.

"Hey, can you show me where to put these clothes I borrowed? I guess Zenia has someone take them to the cleaners and all that."

"Sure thing, follow me," he said.

Damn if we didn't end up right next to the gym where I'd worked out with Xander just a week or so before. God, it seemed like a lifetime ago.

"Thanks, man," I said to Sean. "Hey, do you know if Zenia's in?"

"She's not."

"Do you think we could go somewhere and talk?" I asked.

Sean led the way to Zenia's pristine office, where we settled in. "What's going on, Will?" Sean asked.

"You know the gig I just finished up in Santa Barbara? The multi-day one?" I filled him on the whole long, sordid, almost surreal story. "So after punching him right in the fucking kisser, I said my goodbyes, bounced to a motel overnight, and then came straight here."

I figured I'd be fired. Hell, I figured I could end up shot. But to his credit, Sean was unfazed. At least on the outside.

He leaned forward in his chair, elbows resting on the knees of his perfectly tailored pants. "First, I want to say, I'm sorry you went through all that. And I'm surprised Zenia gave you that as one of your first assignments. I mean, I get it, but…she must have felt you were really perfect for the gig. She saw something in you that told her you would really mesh with the client."

She sure was right about that.

"Sean, the icing on the cake is that I have feelings for Clover, now. It killed me to leave her, even though I knew it was the right thing to do."

He shook his head. "This sort of shit never happens in one shot, does it? Listen, I can understand developing feelings for a beautiful woman after spending five days with her. It's an easy thing to let happen."

I looked down at my hands. "I didn't want it to happen. Believe me. I have a lot going on in my life and have no room for complications."

"Well, Will, your feelings are natural. Completely. But wait until you've been doing this a long while, like I have. It won't be an issue anymore. I guess I'm immune."

He might be immune, but he hadn't met Clover. I doubted any man in his right mind would be immune to her.

"One of the things I'm concerned about, Sean, is whether my actions reflect badly on Player. The second is whether I'll get to keep my job here, and the third is whether or not I'm going to get paid for this gig. I need to know."

It felt good to get it all out in the open.

"Okay. Zenia *will* most likely be concerned about how this reflects on Player, of course. But I seriously doubt she'll want to dismiss you. Man, I've been doing this a while, and to be honest…you're not even the biggest issue I've heard. We've had guys come through here who *really* fucked up their first time out…as in getting the governor's daughter pregnant fuckup. So chill on that. And last, you'll be paid. Whether the whole amount, I don't know. That's a matter of whether the client thinks she doesn't have to pay based on the circumstances."

Clover wouldn't do that. Would she?

"Thanks, Sean. Thank you for listening. I'm going to be honest, though…I'm not sure this escorting thing is right for me."

I really didn't. But one thing I did know—Clover *was* right for me. There was no doubt about that.

CHAPTER 17

CLOVER

"Let's go to the dining room. I'll have Sanders make us some lunch," my mom said, rising from her dressing table, wearing another of her floaty silk numbers. Her eyes were red, which she was clearly trying to hide behind a broad smile and some expensive Chanel powder. But I knew Mom...the more floofy she dressed, the more upset she was.

"Mom," I said, as Jess and I followed her out of her room, "we need to talk."

She waved her hand as if dismissing an annoying fly. "C'mon, girls. We'll have some nice salad for lunch. Maybe with some seared tuna on the side."

I looked at Jess like *what?* She shook her head and shrugged.

"Sanders!" Mom called.

He appeared silently like he always did. The man was definitely part ninja.

I'd known him nearly all my life but didn't know much about him. Never was a big fan of his, but he took good care of my parents and was loyal. I wasn't sure what he thought of *me* at that point—he undoubtedly knew the whole story of Jess's wedding disaster—but he'd never let on, anyway.

"Yes, Mrs. Lufkin. Ready for some lunch?" he asked as he stood ramrod straight in his trousers, polo shirt, and loafers.

"We are," she said, taking a seat at the long dining table that was always set.

"Coming right up," he said, and disappeared.

We sat silently at the table for a moment, Mom pretending all was well with the world, and Jess and me trying to figure out how to snap her out of her pretend reality.

Sanders set a bottle of chardonnay down on the table. Drinking was the last thing on my mind, but maybe a glass would help Mom relax.

"The house is quiet, Mom. Where's Dad?" Jess asked.

She took a slow and deliberate sip of her wine, and when she set her glass down, she shifted it around on the table as if she were looking for the perfect spot for it. She gazed out the dining room window and answered catatonically. "He's running errands."

Jess and I looked at each other again. If we didn't know

better, we'd have sworn Mom had just popped a few Xanax or something.

Sanders entered and started serving.

"Sanders, do you know where my dad is?" I asked.

"Yes, Clover. He's out dealing with the caterer, and, um, other things."

As soon as he'd left the dining room, I looked at my mother.

"Mom."

Not looking up, she picked at her salad. "This salad is really lovely. I'll have to let Sanders know," she said quietly.

"Mom. Would you please look at me?"

She raised her head and gazed at me. Her eyes were not only now red, but there was also something terrible behind them. She set her fork down slowly and glared at me, and then Jess.

"Mom—"

But she cut me off. "Clover, if you hadn't pulled your little stunt, your sister would be married right now, and our family would not be the laughingstock of our community," she said between clenched teeth.

Jess raised her hand to interrupt. "Mom, hold on one—"

But Mom interrupted her with a pointed finger. "I'll get to you in a minute."

Jess sank back into her chair.

"Mom, if you can't see the huge bullet your daughter just dodged, then I don't even know what to say to you," I said, my voice level but my words blunt.

She nodded. "*You're* the one who doesn't get it."

"You know...I think you're partially right. I *didn't* get that I was just fine without a date, and that I didn't have to pay someone. I *didn't* get that despite your incessant matchmaking, I could have just stood up and told you that The Jester's a fucking creep who spends more time looking at my tits than my eyes. I *didn't* get that I have a say in how I interact with this family. But now I do. I let myself be pressured, because I thought the real me was not good enough."

"Is that what you thought?" she asked.

"It's what I thought. But I don't anymore, Mom."

She looked down at her plate.

I leaned toward her, hoping my words would penetrate her anger. "I'm sorry I lied. I made a mistake, and I won't do it again." I glanced at Jess, who had tears streaming down her face. "But Jess, you're the one owed the biggest apology. I should have been honest with you from the beginning."

Mom sniffed, and anger flared inside me. How did my mother make a situation like Jess's about herself? It was beyond me.

"Mom," Jess started, "if Clover hadn't done what she had, we never would have seen Rob's true colors. She did me—and us—a huge favor."

Mom looked from one of us to the other, again. "I don't know why you girls don't understand the importance of choosing a partner from *our* world."

"Mom, did you hear what you just said?" I asked. "You are suggesting we choose someone with money and connections above all else. Do you know how messed up that is?"

She pursed her lips and took a deep breath. "It's the way—"

"That's not how women choose partners anymore, Mom," I said. "It was a hundred years ago, but women have been kicking down doors and breaking ceilings since even your day. The only people who still insist on that sort of outdated thinking are misogynists, gold diggers, and sluts. You're none of those, Mom. I won't speak for Jess here, but I'm going to say what I believe. Women are enough—we don't need a guy to make us whole. Your ideas might not be completely behind us, but they are fading fast."

Mom pulled a hand over her mouth and squeezed her eyes shut. "I just want you girls to have what I've had with your father."

Jess ran around the table and put her arms around our mother. "Mom, that's what we want, too. But it's not because of this house, or the money, or all the material wealth that he's showered on us. What I want is someone who loves me the way Dad loves you. Dad is a great guy. I'd do anything for someone like him. I don't care where he lives or what kind of car he drives."

Will's face wandered through my thoughts, and a lump grew in my throat. How would I ever manage to forget probably the only guy I'd ever felt I wanted to be with on a long-term basis?

"What's going on here?"

We turned to find Dad in the doorway.

"Oh, Dad," I said, running to him. I threw my arms around his neck, and in the way he hugged me back, I knew that, at least for my father, things were okay. He hugged me, and I was for a moment his little girl again.

"Okay, okay. We've all had enough drama for one day," he said.

I took him by the hand and led him to a seat at the table just as Sanders poked his head into the room.

"Sir, can I get you some lunch?" he asked, completely unfazed by the emotions on display.

"That'd be great, Sanders." Dad reached his hand out for one of my mother's. "Patsy. You okay?" he asked.

She dabbed at her tears with a napkin and sniffed. "Yes, Hart. I think everything will be fine."

"You know, Jessamyn and Clover, when your mother met me, she had no idea who I was," Dad said.

She looked up at him with a little smile.

"She'd missed her ride home from a party and asked me for a lift." He glanced over at her with a look anyone would kill to get from his or her love.

He really was quite the catch.

"I told her she'd have to ride on the back of my motorcycle. I don't think she was too happy about that, but it was late at night, and everyone else at the party was blotto drunk. There weren't any other options."

"Wait...Daddy owned a motorcycle?" Jess asked, and I had to agree with her. My father wasn't a stick in the mud, but imagining him on a motorcycle of all things...whoa.

The hardness had left my mother's eyes. "It's true. I

knew nothing about him. He drove me home and asked for my number. We went out for months before I realized he didn't just work for an aircraft company—he and his father *owned* it."

"So basically Mom, you hit the jackpot," I said.

Her back stiffened and she rolled her eyes. "I don't know whether I'd put it like that."

Mom had landed not only a man who was on his way to being wildly successful, but who also was just plain awesome.

That didn't happen every day.

"Mom, Jess and I want the same chance you had at love. That's all. And we'll find it. You just have to stop pressuring us," I said.

"So all this," she said, waving her arms around, "is my fault."

"Patsy," Dad said, leaning toward her and taking both her hands, "Clover doesn't mean that. But she has a point. I've said it before, but you kept insisting I'm an idiot on this. The girls will find their own way."

I planted a big kiss on my father's face.

"Now, Clover. I know you had a, um, special arrangement with Will," Dad said.

My face burned with shame, and I nodded. "I'm sorry, Dad."

He turned to me, my favorite guy ever with his salt and pepper hair and craggy, lined face from years of boating, and said, "Any chance we might see a bit more of him? I mean, anyone who's on the honor roll at UCLA gets the thumbs up from me. And the man's got a mean hook that defended my daughter's honor, too."

Wait? What?

I took a deep breath to calm my voice, which was going to get shaky at any moment. "I don't think so, Dad. I'm not sure that's an option."

He reached for my hand. It was amazing how connected we'd always been. I had no doubt he knew the depth of my feelings for Will and the pain I was suffering over losing him.

"Clover," Jess said, "he really was a great guy."

"And so handsome, too," my mother said. "Even if he was a little...rough around the edges."

"I know. You guys, seriously. I know." I took the hanky my dad handed me and blew my nose.

"I have something to say," Jess said, looking around the table. When she had everyone's attention, she continued. "I want to apologize for bringing Rob and his horrible family into our lives. It was a big mistake."

I'd always known Rob was a creep, but I'd underestimated exactly how low he'd go. We all had.

We'd known their family forever but not really spent any time with them until Jess started bringing Rob around. My parents tolerated the Van Newsoms because they were polite and didn't want to cause waves for Jess. And Mom, I'm sure, was relieved to have Jess 'safely married into a good family.' But maybe they should have spoken up more.

And now, I could kick myself for not speaking my own mind earlier. I could have saved us all some trouble. I knew that back when, from the way that Rob looked at me, his fiancé's *sister*, that he was no good. On more than one occasion after that, I'd caught him staring at my boobs or butt and had overheard him talking to one of his friends over the phone.

"Yeah, getting together with Jessamyn's family this weekend. Her hot as shit sister will be there. Can't wait," he'd said.

Who the hell talks about their girlfriend's sister that way?

Of course I told no one. Maybe I should have. But it didn't matter anymore.

What *did* matter was my next move. I sat back in my chair while Dad and Jess mused about a family vacation someplace far away and exotic, which they thought would help us all clear our heads. I stirred the coffee Sanders had brought us and pulled my buzzing phone out of my pocket.

Someone was calling from Player.

I slipped my phone back into my pocket. I'd call them later.

I had to figure out what I wanted to say, first.

CHAPTER 18

WILL

"**W**hy don't you tell me what happened," Zenia said when I'd caught her in her office early in the morning. She looked amazing as always, perfectly composed and perfectly comfortable in flattering designer denim, a peach colored silk T-shirt, and black jacket.

A professional to the core, she showed no reaction while I shared the story of how Rob had outed me and embarrassed the entire Lufkin family. When I finished, instead of yelling at me like I still somewhat expected, she shook her head sadly.

"I'm sorry, Will. Sorry you went through that, especially that early in your employment with Player. I wish you'd exhibited more self-control and just exited the situation, but I understand a man can only take so much." Her face broke into a huge grin, and she leaned forward on her desk, perfectly manicured hands folded. "Buuut—"

"Yes?"

She leaned forward and lowered her voice conspiratorially. "If you hadn't decked him, I'm not sure I'd be able to respect you."

Whew. That was a huge weight off my shoulders.

"I appreciate your support. Thank you."

"I appreciate your honesty and your integrity," she said in a boss–employee sort of way that felt good—not condescending. Who knew an escort agency would be run by the epitome of professionalism?

She continued. "Sean shared with me you were concerned about whether or not you would be paid. You will be, but there won't be any bonus. I'm sorry about that."

I couldn't complain.

She stood and walked around the desk toward me, and I was struck again at how the soft peach tone of her shirt set off her glowing brown skin. Maybe I was starting to develop a little bit of a taste for the finer things? Nah... Zenia was just the sort of woman who could wear a paper bag and make it look amazing.

"Are you up for another assignment, Will? Maybe something a bit more low-key, this time?" she asked with a smile. "I promise, it's one of Xander's former clients, and she's a total sweetheart. Eighty-seven, long widowed, and just likes to have company to the opera?"

I looked down at my hands, uncertain how I wanted to answer the question I knew I'd eventually be asked.

"Can I get back to you on that? I'm not sure I'm ready yet. And I have to straighten out a couple things with my little sister."

I glanced at my watch and realized I'd be late for the taco lunch I'd promised Chili if I didn't get a move on.

Xenia nodded, unfazed. "How are things with your sister, Will? Sandy and Rich told me they'd spent a bit of time with her. They're very fond of her."

I nodded my head slowly. "And she adores them. Especially Sandy. I don't know how I'll ever thank them. They're good guys."

I must have done something right, because Zenia gave me a sisterly hug after she'd walked me to the door. She'd never done that before, at least not to me. I couldn't overemphasize how awesome it was to have her vote of confidence.

And Sean had been right. I was getting paid in full. That money from my gig with Clover was going to make a huge difference in Chili's and my lives. I almost wanted to say it meant the world. But there was something...*someone* else that *really* meant the world to me. And I was trying my hardest to let it go.

My phone buzzed with a call from my sis, and while I swiped it open, I ran past a snapshot of Clover I'd grabbed when we were at the pool. Her lush tits were covered in the thinnest of bikini material, and her lightly tanned skin was dotted in beaded water from our swim. Her head was tilted, and her aviators reflected back at me taking her photo.

I swiped my phone open to see what Chili was up to. But when I said *hello*, she wasn't there.

Butt dial, I guessed.

I pulled my car into traffic to head the short distance to UCLA. I hadn't been on campus since I'd moved all my crap back home and had had a lot of loose ends to tie up— not least of which was to straighten out my overdue account. With the money I'd earned from my gig with Clover, I could pay what I owed them and set myself up for the coming semester. It'd be tough, but I was more determined than ever to finish up my degree on time and show Chili how it was done.

At least something good had come from my time with Clover.

My phone buzzed, and I pressed the button on my steering wheel to answer it.

"Is this Mr. Will Adams?" an official-sounding voice asked.

Another bill collector, maybe? It was all good though. I was on the road to getting things stable for Chili and me. Plus, it was a gorgeous L.A. day.

"Yes, this is Will Adams. How can I help you?"

That's when I got a punch to the stomach.

"Mr. Adams, your sister, Charlene Adams, has been in an accident."

"*What?*" I swerved in traffic, and an oncoming Prius laid

on its horn while jerking out of the way. Shit, dude, hold it together.

"Sir, can you come to the UCLA medical center right away?"

I stomped on the accelerator and blasted through a yellow light.

"I'm on my way. Is she okay? What happened?" I demanded.

Papers shuffled in the background. "We can fill you in when you arrive, Mr. Adams. We'll see you soon."

Goddammit. Those fuckers could have told me more than they did.

Terror washed over me so sharply that it was all I could do to keep from getting sick. I was instantly transported back to the day I'd found out about my parents' deaths.

This couldn't be happening again. It just couldn't. Life would never be that unfair.

Would it?

I ran my car up to the curb at the emergency room, ignoring the attendant who came out to say something, and dashed inside the hospital. I even left my engine on. Tow it, impound it, for all that it mattered. Chili was the only thing that mattered.

A nurse in blue scrubs looked up from her computer, full of concern when she saw the panic on my face. "Yes?"

"You have a patient named Charlene Adams? I'm her brother," I forced out, unable to make any more sound. I had to remind myself to breathe.

She jumped up from her chair. "Come with me, please."

I don't know how I got from point A to point B, that's how my mind was racing. Was Chili...okay? I couldn't even think about the alternative.

I followed the fast-walking nurse until she pushed open a big, swinging door. There, swallowed up by a huge hospital bed, was my little Chili, a cut across her forehead and bruising under one of her eyes.

"Will," she whispered, extending her hand in my direction.

I grabbed her hand and knelt by the side of her bed. The nurse scooted a chair over to me, and I turned to her. "Is she going to be all right? What happened?" I demanded.

"She's banged up but should be fine. Apparently she was out joyriding with some friends." The nurse put her hands on her hips and shook her head. "Your sister's a very lucky girl, Mr. Adams. She's sedated now but will be fine."

She signaled with her head for me to follow her out of the room.

I kissed Chili on the unharmed side of her forehead. "I'll be right back. I'm just going to talk to the nurse."

Her eyes fell closed, and she nodded weakly.

When we were outside, the nurse laid it out for me. "Mr. Adams, one of the kids in the car has a broken jaw." She looked down, shaking her head. "The other didn't make it."

The beige hospital walls were suddenly dotted with red circles, and my head felt ready to explode. I dropped back against the wall.

"Here. Sit," said the nurse, grabbing a chair. "Let me get you some water."

"Who was driving?" I managed to whisper when she returned.

She shook her head. "We don't know yet. Would you like to see a doctor?"

I pushed myself up, taking deep breaths until the world came into focus again. I had to get back to Chili. "No, I'll be fine. Thank you."

I went back to the quiet, dimly lit room where Chili was and sat next to her again. I smoothed back the dark hair that looked so much like my mother's and watched her chest rise and fall as she slept.

I woke with a wicked crook in my neck from having fallen asleep with my head on the edge of Chili's bed. It was dark outside, I had no idea what time it was, but when I took her hand, she made a small whimper.

"Chili? Chili, are you awake, sweetie?"

Her eyes fluttered open, and she looked at me for a moment. "Hi," she whispered.

"Are you okay? Do you need anything?" I asked.

"Water? Can I have some water?"

I poured some water from the pitcher on her night-stand and brought it to her lips.

"Chili, what happened? What caused the accident?"

My heart broke that sooner or later, she'd find out one of her friends hadn't made it. But I wasn't going to tell her just then.

"I went for a ride," she said, taking a rest. "These kids from school were driving and..." She looked toward the window, where we could see the sunrise.

"I...I don't remember what happened. It's weird, but I don't remember." She looked at me with terrified eyes.

I badly wanted to comfort her but wasn't sure how. I thought about what my father would have done. I needed him. I really needed him.

"I'm sure it's normal to not remember. Don't worry. Just focus on feeling better. I'm here for you."

She dozed off again, and to my relief, I was able to join her, sore neck be damned.

Sleeping was a welcome respite for us both, seeking a desperate break from the real world, which had suddenly become too much to bear.

"Mr. Adams. Mr. Adams," a voice said, shaking me by the shoulder. Eventually, I opened my eyes to find a nurse hovering over me and Chili lying on her side, smiling.

"Mr. Adams, you can take your sister home now," she said.

"Yeah, Will. My medicine wore off. I'm ready to leave." Chili reached for my arm and shook me to help get the sleep out of my head.

I pushed my fingers through my hair in an attempt to address my bed head. "Wow. I was sound asleep."

I turned to Chili. "You feel well enough to leave?"

She nodded with enthusiasm. "I'm starving. And I don't want the food here."

The nurse agreed. "There's no reason to keep her any longer. But you'll want to follow up with your family doctor in a few days. If you'll excuse us, Mr. Adams, I'll help your sister get dressed."

I stepped outside, counting my lucky stars. Life wasn't perfect, and there were going to be some big speed bumps ahead, but it could be a whole hell of a lot worse.

"Looks like you're finally getting your tacos," I told Chili as I drove to our favorite place.

I walked around to her side of the car to help her out. "You seem pretty stiff. Maybe when we get home you should soak in the tub."

She looked up at me as I helped her to the taco stand. "That's just what Mom would have said."

Well. That felt damn nice.

"Why don't you sit at the picnic bench over here and I'll order for you?" I asked. It was a gorgeous day, and eating outside would be just the ticket.

"Okay. You know what I like."

While I waited in line, I thought of all the times we'd been to that very taco joint with our parents. Since we were little we'd been going there. And now it was Chili and me. Just us two.

I returned to the table, where Chili had her bruised face

turned to the sun. She was catching some looks from other diners but was happily oblivious. "Here are your two carnitas tacos, with black beans and pico de gallo, and here are mine, two grilled chicken with the works. I also got us some chips and guac."

Chili pushed her hair off her forehead and winced when she brushed the stitches on her forehead. "You're a good brother, Will," she said as a little sob escaped her mouth.

"Thank you. I try," I said, diving into my food.

"That accident…I don't know how it happened. I have to find out what happened to the other kids," she said, her face crossed with concern. "I'd call them, but I lost my phone in the accident."

"We will," I reply, knowing that she'd have to face the hard truth eventually. I was not looking forward to that. "We'll find out. For now, let's just chow and then get you home." I patted my pocket where the nurse had given me Chili's phone, found at the accident and returned by the police.

I wasn't sure how to break the news to her, but I didn't have to worry about that just then.

"How is your bodyguard job?" she asked, piling a huge lump of guacamole onto a too-small chip.

"Oh, it's okay, I think. Not sure when I'll have another one. I want to get our custody hearing out of the way and then get myself set up to return to classes next semester. I'm so close to graduating."

"Well, whoever you were working for in Santa Barbara must have loved you."

What the hell was she talking about?

"Why do you look so surprised? Will, you're a seriously hunky guy. You know, all my friends are in love with you," she said teasingly.

"Gee, thanks. Just what I always wanted. A bunch of sixteen-year-olds in love with me."

She leaned over the table toward me and lowered her voice. "Don't look, but there's a very pretty woman over there staring at you."

"Yeah, right. Eat your tacos so we can get you home and to bed."

She peered over my shoulder again. "I'm not kidding. She's wearing Converse Chucks. She has long, dark hair—"

Holy shit.

I spun around to find the lovely Clover—the woman I'd not been able to get off my mind for a moment—at the picnic bench behind me, smiling and looking more beautiful than ever. When I got my wits back, I stood, frozen in place. We stared at each other, and then she ran, throwing herself into my arms.

And she smelled damn good.

"What the hell? How did you find me?" I asked. "Oh, by the way, this is Chili. Chili, meet Clover."

Clover extended her hand. "I've heard a lot about you."

"Really? You have?" She beamed, her injuries seemingly forgotten. She was instantly smitten with Clover, like she'd just found the big sister she'd always searched for and never had. "You're so pretty."

"Thank you… Did something happen to you, sweetie?" Clover asked, looking at Chili's stitches and bruises, then back up at me.

Chili rolled her eyes. Back to her teenage snark, which I guessed that was a good sign. "Oh, it's nothing," she said, dramatically waving her hand in the air.

"Well. Okay." Clover looked at me. "You'd told me you and your sister like this taco place. I drove by to check it out and saw your Jeep."

She was so casual and down-to-earth with nothing more than something glossy and barely pink on her lips. It was hard to believe we were out on her father's yacht just a couple days earlier.

I glanced at Chili, who was listening to our every word.

"In case you're wondering, Chili was in an accident. But she's going to be fine. In fact, we should probably head home," I said. I turned away before my heart could break again, but Chili had other plans.

"Why don't you come with us, Clover? We can watch a movie together. At least until I pass out," she said with a giggle. "Probably won't take me too long."

Christ, she was a smart little bugger. She knew me far better than I thought she did.

Clover looked at me, and I nodded, taking her hand and surrendering to fate. I wasn't going to run from her again. Instead, I was going to hang onto her with whatever it took. Seeing her there, right in front of me, I was struck with the truth. She was worth every sacrifice and every effort to keep her in my life. This time, I wasn't letting her go so easily.

"Sounds good. Let's go."

CHAPTER 19

CLOVER

I was back in Will's arms, and I'd never felt so good.

His adorable little sister, even though she'd just been in the hospital, asked if she could spend the night over at Mrs. Jones's, their neighbor. I guess she was like a second mother of sorts to the kid, because Will caved after a few minutes of her begging. I suspected Chili read the vibes between us a lot better than she let on. So after packing a backpack, she kissed Will on the cheek and bounced, humming happily.

"Now you see where I live," he said after she'd gone, pouring us each a glass of wine as we settled onto the living room sofa.

It was a comfortable house. Warm and lived-in. I could tell it had once been full of love. Hell it still *was* full of love. I looked around at the family photos and other mementos of lives well lived, and realized that it was, in its own way, just as beautiful as my family home with its acres of land, guest cottages, and pool. All a home really needed was pure, unadulterated family love.

"It's great. A wonderful home," I reassured him, snuggling in tight. "I love it. And I can't believe I'm here, with you."

He picked my hand up and kissed the back of it softly.

"Hey, did your sis vacate to give us privacy?" I asked, just to see if my suspicions were correct.

A slight smile crossed his handsome face, and he pushed his hair back by raking it with his fingers. "I suspect she did. I mean, she loves staying over at Mrs. Jones's. Ever since my parents passed, Mrs. Jones has been looking out for Chili. Kind of took her under her wing. Helps her with homework, etcetera. But yeah, I suspect she wanted to clear out for us. Funny kid, how she picks up on things."

A serious looked washed over his face. "I'm fighting to get custody of her. If I don't, she may end up in foster care."

It felt like someone had just knocked the wind out of me. Good god, no wonder he'd turned to the job he'd taken. "No, they can't do that. No one will look after her better than you do."

He dropped his head into his hand and squeezed his eyes tightly shut. "I know. I just have to prove to the courts that it's in her best interest to remain with me, in our house. Well, I also have to keep her out of trouble. Which is proving to be a challenge." He took a swig of his wine and shook his head. "She's got a wild side, and I'm sure this is just a hint of the teenage rebellion to come."

Setting his glass down, he turned to me. "Clover, I have a couple things to say, and I'm going to just get them off my chest since you're here."

My heart pounded. Shit. I shouldn't have stalked him. Shouldn't have tracked him down. He was going to say that I was a psycho, and that while he liked me fine for a few days, that was the extent of it, and that I needed to hit the road and never look back—

He took one of my hands. It had been only a few days, but I'd desperately missed the way he looked at me. "Since I left Santa Barbara, you haven't been out of my thoughts for more than five minutes."

The tears. I could feel them coming. Dammit. Guess he didn't think I was a psycho.

"When I took the assignment to be with you, I'd assumed you'd be some snotty, stuck-up brat with daddy issues. Instead, I don't think I've ever met anyone I've felt more comfortable with. And yet we come from such different worlds."

I could see why he'd said that. I guess it was why, the first time we'd met, I'd made such an effort to look like such a plain Jane. Or was I really just trying to convince myself that I was just like everybody else?

He continued. "I'm sorry for punching out Rob. That was not the best way to handle that situation. I could have taken the high road and just quietly left."

Thank god he *didn't*. "Are you serious? It was one of the

most satisfying things in my life to see that prick get what was coming to him." Actually, I wished there had been more pummeling. It would have been so delicious.

I touched his face with gentle fingers. "And, before you can continue, you should know...there were a lot of good things to come out of your kicking his ass. If it wasn't for you, we might not have seen Rob's true colors until it was too late, until after he'd married my sister and really gotten a foothold in my family. And guess what—Jess stood him up at the altar."

Will stood up and whoop-whooped, leaving me laughing. "So, the fake date, also known as *me*, saved the day, more or less?"

"I'd say so. And another thing..."

"Yeah?" he asked.

"The fake date was quite a hit with the family, but even more so with me. I'm afraid I'm falling for the fake date. No...not falling. Fall*en*."

There. I'd said it out loud, for the first time. And hopefully not the last.

And Will smiled.

I sensed the feeling was mutual

We retired to Will's bedroom, still buried in boxes since his move back home after the accident.

"I like what you've done with the place."

He sat on the edge of his bed and pulled me in until his

head was buried in my shirt, inhaling deeply and humming with satisfaction and happiness.

"Fucking A, I've missed the way you smell." He lifted my T-shirt over my head while I kicked off my sneakers.

In one swift movement he flipped me to my back, on the bed in a tangle of pillows and bed linens. He hovered over me, still fully dressed, a raging hard-on straining the seams of his blue jeans.

I reached for his fly and made quick work of his zipper with my shaking hands. I'd been so afraid I'd never get to touch him again. He was everything...all I wanted, all my soul and heart desired. "I need you. I need you," I murmured.

"Yeah? You need me or my hard cock?" he asked with a smile.

I could only laugh.

I'd *missed* him. It had been only a few days—nothing really, in the long continuum that was life—but it had seemed like an unholy hell of an interval. The sadness that had seeped into my bones over everything that had happened was leaching back out, relieving me of what felt like a thousand pounds of grief. I was glad to let it go.

I shimmied his pants down over his hips, and in a graceful movement, he'd kicked off his own shoes and shaken both to the floor. His shirt came off in a blur, and I pulled him back to me. While his cock pressed against the panties separating our sex, my hands roved through his hair, and I covered his face in kisses. I was voracious, a starving woman seated at a buffet, unable and unwilling to hold back.

My hands reached for the hem of my lace panties, but he took my wrists in his powerful grip, swatting them away. My breath came hard and raspy as he bent to kiss my stomach, then followed the edge of my panties as he pulled them down to bare my pussy. With them still around the tops of my thighs, I was unable to open my legs the way I wanted so I could give him all of myself, but that seemed to be part of his plan.

And who was I to argue?

With my legs pressed tightly together, he ran his finger up and down my bare slit and parted my lips just enough to reach my clit with the tip of his tongue. He tortured me with several flicks, and my pussy ached as blood rushed to my core.

"Will, oh god..." I whimpered. "Fuck you're amazing."

He moaned as his lips zeroed in on my hard nub to form a suction that about sent me through the roof.

"I...want more. Please," I begged.

Something about having been apart for a few days, and afraid I'd never see him again, not to mention the relief of being far away from all that had happened in Santa Barbara, made our reunion surreal. I trembled harder at every touch until an orgasm detonated throughout me. I arched harder into his mouth as violent shudders washed over me.

"You taste so good," he murmured, reaching to the floor for his pants.

He returned with a condom, which he had opened and rolled down his great length in a mere moment. He pulled one of my legs out of my panties, and with his hands under my thighs pushed my legs up until they rested on his shoulders. I was wide open and ready when he stopped what he was doing.

"Are you ready? Are you ready for me, baby?" he asked.

"Yes, please, Will, I'm ready…"

"You're so wet." He pried me slightly open to make way for his cock, and I closed my eyes, making pleading sounds.

He paused, his own breath growing ragged, and plunged inside, my tender flesh making way for his hard pounding. I clenched around every inch of him, my legs in the air as he gripped me for leverage.

"You good, baby?" he asked, his own voice ragged.

My head lolled back on the pillows as I breathed, "Yes, yes, please…"

My pulse roared in my ears, but through it I heard him growl with a potent ferocity, and I knew I was his. He wanted me, and I was giving myself to him to claim and make his own.

He got even bigger, stretching me to my limit as he came in an all-out rut.

I clawed at the bedsheets as he shuddered inside me, gripping my shaking legs before easing them aside and bending to kiss my temple.

We lay naked on top of the bed, Will flat on his back, his body slick with sweat and his cock still semi-erect, resting on the crease where his leg met his hip. His eyes were closed as he caught his breath, and his hand reached blindly until it found mine, which he grasped with tight fingers.

"Fuck, baby," he said. "You are so goddamn amazing."

I gazed at him as I lay on my side. "I might say the same thing about you. I feel like I've been drugged or something. I'm still tingling from head to toe."

He shifted to his side, facing me. "Yeah?" he asked.

I nodded, amazed that it could be even better than it was in Santa Barbara. I'd never thought it possible. "Well, you did kind of just fuck my brains out."

He laughed. "I hope I didn't fuck them all out. I think you'll need them when you get back to the classroom," he said, running his fingers along the length of my torso. He was still flushed and sweaty and had a serious case of bedhead, but his glittering eyes and slight facial scruff were about more than I could take.

I followed his finger as he traced my skin. "Your control is so hot."

The way he held back until I was ready to go was such an undeniable turn-on. I ran my fingers down his chest, past his belly button, and found that he was hard. Again.

"I don't even know how many times I came," I whispered.

He got right next to my ear, and whispered back, "It wasn't enough," and rolled me onto my stomach. He lifted me onto my knees, positioned himself behind me, and rolled on another condom. He notched himself at my opening, always ready.

So was I.

I heard the shower running and realized Will was no longer beside me in bed. Light shone through the window, and I pushed myself up, swinging my legs over the side of the bed to start getting ready for my student teaching gig.

"Hey, you're up," he said, coming back in the room wearing just a towel. He flashed me his heartbreaker smile. That damn dimple. Again.

"You going somewhere?" I asked, walking over to him and releasing his towel. We faced each other, both completely naked.

He pushed my hair back and lifted my chin for a kiss. "I have a few things to take care of today. I need to meet with Zenia at Player and get over to UCLA to talk about next semester."

My emotions were so mixed I stumbled for words.

And Will was so intuitive, it didn't get by him.

"C'mere," he said, leading me to the edge of the bed. He took a seat next to me. "I'm talking to Zenia about retiring...although I guess you can't call it retirement after so short a tenure, could you?"

My head snapped in his direction, and my heart pounded. "Really? Why?"

He took my hand. "Well, it's not something I can do anymore. I have other things to focus on, and it no longer fits into my life."

I didn't want to be a possessive bitch, but I was damn glad to hear that.

"Are you sure?" I asked.

"Yup."

I looked down at my hands and smiled, then looked back up at Will. He didn't say anything. Neither did I.

We didn't need to.

CHAPTER 20

WILL

"Your Honor, I really want to stay with my brother, Will, here. He's really helped me to get my act together."

Chili looked over at me, and I thought how proud my parents would be. Things weren't perfect, but we'd come a hell of a long way in just a few months. It'd been dicey there for awhile, but we were getting it together.

The judge nodded. "Tell me more, Charlene."

"One of my neighbors helped me get a job at a nursery," she said, referring to Mrs. Jones's grown son. "And I've really pulled my grades up, especially in biology. I'm getting an A."

Christ, I was proud of my little sis. Her part-time job had given her a new sense of purpose, reminding me of when I was that age and had a job at a video store. When she realized she could make a little money and found she had quite the green thumb thanks to the plants she got for free at her job, she cut off all of the slacker kids she'd been hanging out with. There was no room left in her life to be a goof-off. 'Course, the car accident had been the most impactful in scaring her straight, so to speak. She knew she'd been lucky, and that the driver had paid with her life for the prank that was the final factor needed in completely changing my sister's outlook.

She also gotten a little taller and more willowy which, truth be told, made me nervous as hell. She turned heads everywhere we went, and I knew it wouldn't be long before I'd have to start screening boyfriends.

"Mr. Adams, do you have anything to add?" the judge asked.

I stood. "Just that our financial situation is more stable. I'm nearly done with my last few courses at UCLA, and we've gotten things worked out with the insurance companies. It's all arranged. I've remained at my parents' house to look after Chili—I mean Charlene—while in school."

I'd seriously done all I could to convince the courts that Chili belonged with me. They wanted us financially solvent, and for her to stay out of trouble and pull up her grades—check, check, check. We were in a groove that no foster family could do better than.

"Charlene. Mr. Adams. I'm very impressed with your dedication to keeping your lives together in the face of the tragedy of losing your parents. And while there are still substantial hurdles in your path, I agree that you two are best off together, rather than being split up. Mr. Adams, I hereby grant you custodianship of your sister, Charlene Adams."

Chili jumped up and down, clapping. "Thank you, thank you so much! Oh, I'm so happy." She threw her arms around me and her tears flowed and there were smiles all around the courtroom.

Shit, even my eyes were filling with tears.

"I can't wait to see Clover. I just love her. She's so beautiful, and smart, and nice…"

There was no understating the liking Chili had taken to Clover. From that very first afternoon in the parking lot by the taco stand, my sister had found a combination super-star and fairy godmother. She spoke of her as if she weren't even mortal. I think she liked Clover better than she liked me.

Which was fine with me. And, I had to say, the admiration went both ways. Sometimes when the two of them were together, it was like there was no one else in the world. Clover was the sister Chili had never had, and the mom she missed so much. And for Clover, it was a chance to help a kid who'd lost nearly everything. I knew the rest of the Lufkins would find the little punk just as enchanting.

Things were falling into place.

~

Chili's head ping-ponged, looking first in one direction at the Pacific Ocean before bouncing over to the other and the mountains above Santa Barbara, like she couldn't decide which direction were more beautiful.

"I've only been here once, on a school trip a long time ago," she said, her eyes wide open, taking it all in. "And that was stupid. They took us to the boring old mission."

I remembered that school trip. It was a big deal that my mom had joined as one of the chaperones. She and Chili had talked about it for years afterward, so I guessed it wasn't *that* stupid. But it reminded me that Chili was still a teenager for a little while, thank god. I had figured out helping her grow up was kind of fun. Most of the time, anyway.

I made the turn up the hill toward Clover's parents' property.

"What's that up there?" Chili asked, pointing. "A hotel or something? It's so pretty."

Seeing the place for the first time was a shocker, no doubt. I remembered my first time there.

"What you're looking at, Chil, is Clover's parents' place."

"*What?*" she shrieked. "No way. That is *not* somebody's house.

"But it is, my friend. Take a deep breath, because you haven't seen anything yet." Despite it being a few months, life had been so busy back in Los Angeles it was only my second time at the Lufkin estate. I'd had a taste of that life for five days when Jessamyn was supposed to get married, but how would it be to live like that every day of your life?

Not sure I wanted to know.

"Why didn't you tell me these people were...I don't even know the word. I guess, rich?" she asked.

I chuckled and looked over at her. "Because, Chili, it really doesn't matter. They're not that different from you and me."

Not sure I really believed that, but it sounded good. "It doesn't matter where Clover and her family live. They've invited us for a long weekend, which is very generous," I said. "And Clover said you can have your very own cottage."

"Wow. Well, I guess I won't be sleeping on a lumpy pull-out sofa in a musty basement rec room, huh?" We both had to laugh at that one.

I pulled into the circular drive, and Sanders was at the door before I'd even set the parking brake.

"Sanders. Nice to see you," I said as I grabbed our bags from the back seat of the Jeep.

"You too, Mr. Will. And you must be Miss Charlene?" he asked. No more nasty glances at my dirty Jeep.

"Hi. I'm *Chili*," my sister said, sticking her hand out. "Are you Clover's dad?"

Amused, Sanders shook his head and took Chili's bag, leading us into the house that I'd thought I'd never see again when I'd last left. Then again, I'd never thought I'd see Clover again, either.

I couldn't say I was returning to the Lufkins without some trepidation. The last time I'd seen them, at the disaster that had been Jessamyn's rehearsal dinner, I'd been called some pretty unflattering things. And despite whatever Clover might have told them since, there had to be bad memories and emotions that were still raw. I knew mine were.

Couldn't say I blamed them. And if they wanted to hang on to those impressions, well, that was their business. The important thing was how Clover felt.

Although I sure did hope to win over her parents.

"There's Clover!" Chili shrieked again. It seemed sixteen-year-olds shrieked a lot. I didn't think I'd ever get used to it.

"Hi, sweetie," Clover said, throwing her arms around my sister. "I missed the hell outta you."

I cleared my throat. "Uh, hello."

"Oh my," Clover said, nudging Chili conspiratorially, "I think your big bro might be a bit jealous of the attention I lavish on you."

"Oh no, he's not jealous, Clover. He knows you love him."

As soon as the words were out of her mouth, Chili's hand flew to her mouth, and she turned pink. But she wasn't the only one. Clover turned beet red, too.

"All right, all right. Calm down you two red-faces." I brushed over Chili's outburst but was pleased as hell that she'd spilled the beans.

"Well, if it isn't the man who punched out the creep my

daughter almost married," Hart bellowed, making Chili jump as she turned around. "Get over here!"

I extended my hand, which he ignored, pulling me into a huge bear hug.

"Great to see you, Hart."

He turned to my sister. "And if this isn't the beautiful young Chili, I'll eat my hat."

Chili beamed. I hadn't realized how much she missed having parent figures. She extended her hand, thought better of it, and threw her arms around Hart.

"Nice to meet you, Mr. Lufkin. Thank you for inviting me. Your place is insane. I've never seen anything like it…" she babbled, and somehow Hart kept track of what she was saying. Practice, I figured, from having raised two daughters.

Either way, it gave me a moment to focus on my girl, who was freshly showered, wearing a snug-fitting sweater and long skirt that swirled when she walked. It had only been the night before that she'd come to Santa Barbara, but it felt like we'd been apart forever. I ran my fingers through the wet tangle of hair that spilled down her back and pulled her to me for a long, lush kiss. I didn't care who saw us.

"Hey, hey, over there. Why don't you two get a room," Jessamyn called as she joined us. In two seconds she'd pried me out of her sister's arms for a quick hug. "Howya doin', stud?"

And right behind was their mother. "Patsy. Good to see

you." She planted a kiss on my cheek, always the restrained one in the family.

Chili turned to say hello. "Hi, Mrs. Lufkin. Gosh, you're so pretty. Just like Clover. And Jessamyn!"

"Thank you, sweetie," Pasty said. "You're a very pretty young lady yourself."

"Thank you, Mrs. Lufkin. And thank you for having me." Then, she looked around wildly. "Will, I can't believe you got to be a bodyguard in this place. It's so awesome!"

Four curious faces swiveled in my direction, question marks on all of them. Jessamyn, who was out of Chili's line of sight, mouthed *bodyguard?* and I knew I'd have to face some teasing over that little fib.

I cleared my throat. "Um, yeah, Chil. It was quite the opportunity."

Clover clasped my hand, and her sister and parents wore amused smiles. They had my back. Just like real family.

For about the tenth time that day, I wondered how I got so damn lucky. Just a few months ago, it felt like the world was closing in around me. I couldn't deny it—those were dark days. Never in a million years did I think I might be where I was at that moment in the Lufkin's house in Santa Barbara, holding hands with my love.

Shit. Did I say *love?* Christ I was turning into a pussy.

Chili threw her arms around Clover like she might never let go. "Clover, I love that outfit! It's so pretty. Do you think I could wear it sometime?"

"Chili…" I warned.

But Clover just laughed. "Sure, Chili. Hey, want Jess and me to show you around the place?"

My sister jumped up and down, clapping her hands.

"When you girls are back, we'll have some lunch out in the sunroom," Patsy called after them.

"You have a *sunroom*? No way!" I heard Chili exclaim as their voices faded. "Hey, Will told me you have a pool, too. Do you think we swim later? I mean, I know it's cold but…?"

Hart shook his head, laughing. "She's a sweetheart, Will. Good kid."

I took a deep breath. "Thanks, Hart. It hasn't been easy, but I think we're on a good track now."

He put a hand on my back. The man wasn't nearly my height, but his presence and personality more than made up for any of his vertical challenges.

"Hey, Will, do you have a moment to chat? We could go into my library. Maybe have a sip of scotch?"

My stomach fell. This was the conversation I'd been dreading and was hoping I could avoid. But I knew better. The man was going to tell me it was all fine and good to pay his home a visit, but after the weekend, he'd expect me —and Chili—to hit the road and sever ties with his daughter.

I knew it in my bones. Couldn't say I blamed him. If I had a daughter, hell, I don't think I'd want her with a man like me.

Fuck. It was going to be hard on Clover. And Chili.

And *me*.

To be honest, I'd practiced what I would say when a conversation like that was on the table. I'd remain calm and assure Hart I only wanted the best for his daughter. That she was a wonderful and unique woman who deserved the best life could offer. That I'd hoped she'd find everything she wanted and dreamed of.

And that there was a spot in there, for me.

True to form, Hart poured us each a small scotch on the rocks. "It's good to see you back here, Will."

I'd rather get the pleasantries out of the way and get down to business. But I was a patient man. "Thank you, Hart."

"Have a seat," he said, pointing to a crackly old leather club chair opposite the sofa where he was perched. "I think your sister's going to have a fun weekend."

Was he kidding? They'd probably never get rid of her.

"I can tell you, she's thrilled to see Clover's childhood home, and before the weekend is out, I'm sure she'll be in love with Jessamyn, too."

He smiled, a man clearly content with his lot in life. He deserved his happiness, no doubt about it.

"How are things otherwise, Will?" he asked pointedly, setting his drink down on the table between us. "I haven't pried much, but I've been curious."

I wasn't sure what he was getting at. And it didn't really matter. "Things are good, Hart. Really good, actually. The biggest thing is that I finally got custody of my sister."

He broke out in a huge grin. "Well, now that is good

news. Congratulations. Well done," he said, holding his glass in toast to me.

"Thank you. All I've got left for next semester is my internship capstone course. I just couldn't do it this semester while taking care of Chili. It'll be great to get all that behind me. I'll also be helping my friends with their food truck business again. They've had a couple investors interested, if you can believe it. They want to franchise food trucks." I shook my head. The world was crazy.

"Impressive. Very impressive. You know, I've been thinking of starting up a leasing program for private jets."

He still hadn't dropped the bomb. But it was coming, no doubt, and I couldn't wait. "What are you getting at, Hart?"

"Why, it's pretty simple. You just said you need an internship, right? And I need some fresh, new entrepreneurial blood at my company. What would you say to coming to work for me? I mean, you'd have to work your way up, no special favors. You're going to have to put in the same blood, sweat, and tears as every other newbie at Lufkin Aircraft. Besides, truth be told...I'd like to keep the company in the family if I can."

Wait. *What did he just say?*

If I wasn't mistaken, the man had just acknowledged my relationship with his daughter. And he had, in some slip of tongue that had to be high on the all time WTF list, said I was family.

Had I heard him right?

"Um...yeah...um, Hart could you repeat that please?"

The scotch was obviously playing games with my hearing, although I'd only taken a sip.

"Will, I'm asking you to come to work for me next semester, and if the fit's right, when you've finished school."

"Oh. Right. Well. I'll have to weigh that against all the other opportunities I'm sure I'll be offered."

The look on his face, of pure shock, was priceless.

I burst out laughing. "Hart! Of course, I'd love nothing more than to come work for your company. What an honor. Holy shit." I jumped to my feet, put my hands on my head, and spun in a circle.

Then I stopped. "Wait. Tell me, does Clover know about this? Is she behind the offer? Because if she is—"

Hart held his hand up like a *stop* sign. "She knows nothing. This is between you and me. Once you are ready, you can tell her."

A sound outside the window caught my attention, and I turned to see the girls outside, talking and laughing, Chili charming the pants off everyone in her wake. She was magical, that one.

"Hart, I gotta level with you. I spent the first month after I last saw you guys swearing you'd be telling me to take a hike because…well, you know," I said, laying it out. It needed to be said, and there was no reason to wait. "And thanks for covering for me on the bodyguard lie. God, I have no idea how I'm going to ever tell Chili how I really met Clover."

His face became serious. How could it not?

"Will, if you want my advice, you tell her the truth. Because all that matters is that you're a man of integrity who treats my daughter like a princess and steps up to the plate when life calls for it. The other things are…well, just details."

I took a deep breath. "What about all your family and friends who know? Do you have concerns about that?"

He pressed his lips together hard before he spoke. "No. No, I do not. If they're going to judge my family, well they can just"—lowering his voice, he looked around—"go fuck themselves."

I couldn't have said it better myself.

"Oh, one more thing," Hart said as he leaned back. "If you take the offer…I'm forcing you to get a pilot's license. I am not having an executive intern for my company who can't fly a plane."

CHAPTER 21 & OTHER STUFF

CLOVER

I was letting my hair fly out the window on a gorgeous day in Northern California's Napa Valley, the hub of California wine country, where I was driving my parents' car to the nearby private airfield. My pulse thrummed in anticipation of seeing Will. It had been only a week—I'd come up to Napa early along with Chili, public school having wrapped up for the year, while he put the finishing touches on his final semester at UCLA—but it could have been an eternity with the way I ached for him.

And now he sprinted down the steps of one of my father's private jets, my heart zooming into overdrive as he scanned the airstrip looking for me. Damn, but he was a handsome devil, turning heads from every direction with his graceful, confident stride. Of course, it didn't hurt that he had the physique of a lifelong athlete and was devastatingly handsome, to boot. His thick black hair ruffled in the light breeze, and he waved when he found me. I grinned like a total idiot, mesmerized to the point where my feet were glued to the asphalt pavement.

"My girl," he murmured, placing the kind of lush kiss on my lips that I'd dreamed of every night we'd been apart. "I've never been to this part of the state. It's freaking beautiful. Hey, has Chili been behaving?"

Even if his little sister hadn't been, I wouldn't rat out the kid. With some of the money she'd earned at her part-time nursery job, she'd insisted on taking my family out for Chinese food the night before. She'd glowed with pride as she paid the bill and tip in cash from the bright Vera Bradley wallet that had been her mother's. My parents hadn't wanted to let her pay, but Will pointed out ahead of time how important it was for Chili to feel she could do something nice for us and share the fruits of her hard work moving and repotting plants for Mrs. Jones's son. It was beyond precious.

She was the kind of girl I hoped to have one day.

She'd also finished out her own year with all A's and one B. She'd never had a report card like that before and was on top of the world knowing it was within her reach. It was cute, how proud Will was of her.

"You know your sister is an angel," I said, wrapping my arm in his as we made our way to the car.

"Okay, I know she actually is not an angel, but I'll let you delude yourself as long as you care to." He stopped and looked around. We were in the valley, but in every direction you looked were mountains and hills, nearly every inch covered with vineyards. What had started out as an industry originated by a few immigrants who'd sneaked vines out of 'the old country' when they'd crossed oceans to get to the United States, had grown into one of the biggest industries in the state of California. There was still plenty of debate about whether California wines held their own compared to those from countries that had been making wines for several hundreds of years, but I was biased toward them. I always would be.

"Hey, you'll get to meet Jess's new boyfriend. He's really super. Worlds away from that asshole Rob." I pulled onto the country road that would take us to my parents' place.

I loved watching him look out the window. I'd been coming to Napa all my life, but I was never tired of seeing the perfectly pruned vines run up and down the hills for as far as the eye could see.

"Oh really?" he said. "Nice guy?"

"He is. You two will get along. He's on a triathlon team. He's actually someone she'd known for a long time. I guess there was always a bit of an attraction there, but with Rob in the picture, neither of them could act on it." It was amazing, actually. I'd never seen my sister happier or more comfortable in her own skin.

It was nearing dinnertime when Will and I returned to the house from the long hike we'd taken among the vineyards.

I'd snapped a ton of photos of him with my phone, which he protested against, of course, but which he also looked smashing in. Go figure.

When we arrived at the table, Chili ran to give her brother a hug. The rest of the family was genuinely thrilled that he'd finished his studies and had also loaned us his lively sister. There were few dull moments with a sixteen-year-old in the house. I'd forgotten what it was like. We all had.

"So what do you think of Napa, so far?" my mother asked.

He inhaled deeply. "It's gorgeous. And the air smells great. You're so fortunate to have this place."

Conversation buzzed around the dinner table, but I just picked at my food, not because I didn't like it, but because I was so excited to be in the same room again with my guy. When dessert rolled around, however, I decided to make an exception. I always was a sucker for tiramisu. We'd each been served a generous slice, when Will cleared his throat and stood at his seat.

I figured he was going to toast my parents for inviting him and Chili. I loved his exquisite manners. I beamed proudly. I just couldn't help it.

I looked around the table at how much my family had changed in less than a year. Jess was with a man who treated her with respect, and who had integrity by the barrelful. And I had a boyfriend who came with a charming and hilarious sidekick.

My parents smiled at each other and took each other's

hand. Even *they* seemed like their always-happy marriage had been somehow rejuvenated.

Will held a glass of dessert wine in his hand. "Thank you, Patsy and Hart, for inviting my sister and me up here to your incredible wine country home. It's an honor to have been included."

Everyone around the table wore gigantic smiles, including me.

He looked down at me. "I wanted to include all of you in a special request I'm making of my love, here."

Um. What?

And don't you know, he pulled a little box out of his sweatshirt pocket. The kind of box that held a ring.

What the fucking fuck?

A noise caught my attention, and all our heads turned toward the end of the table. Chili had her hand over her mouth, from which had just escaped a loud sob. Her shoulders shook, wracked with emotion.

Okayyyy…

Will walked around the table and pulled me to my feet. I glanced nervously at everyone.

His gaze was unwavering. "I have something for you. It's a promise to work toward the kind of happy relationship your parents have and that my parents once had."

I took the box and pried open the lid. Inside was a delicate gold band with a tiny chip of a diamond.

It was the most beautiful thing I'd ever seen.

"I have a question for you," Will said.

A lump built in my throat, but I pushed past it. "Is it about making life perfect?" I asked.

He laughed. "No, it is definitely not about making life perfect. We both know that is not humanly possible."

Now the tears were rolling down my face. The others at the table were just a big blur, but I could swear I saw my mom and Jess dabbing at their eyes with their white cloth napkins. And of course, Chili continued to make all manner of racket at her end of the table.

"I mean, babe," Will said, looking around the table, too. "I'd like to work toward that goal, but are we ready? For perfection, I mean?"

I pushed a tear off my face. "We'll never be ready for perfection, because it doesn't exist. But I'd be willing to die trying."

"I'd be honored to die trying with you, my love."

With his hands on either side of my face, he pulled me in for a passionate kiss. Applause erupted from all around the table, and as always, Chili got the last word.

"Clover's going to be my sister! For real!"

She leapt out of her chair, screaming and jumping up and down.

Will leaned close to my ear. "I hope you're okay that this is a package deal."

"It's more than okay." I said.

"It's perfection."

Get a free short story!

Join my Insider Group

IF you liked *Mister Fake Date*, check out this excerpt from:
Mister Wrong
A Player Romance, Book 3

DOVE

I was vexed. Shaking with rage. All because of a little brat.

Who actually, at eighteen years old, wasn't all that little. But she sure as hell acted the fool, snapping her gum and rolling her eyes—right in my face. The ponytail positioned on the very top of her head and gobs of black eyeliner trying to achieve the trendy 'wings' look didn't add to her maturity, either.

Yup, just another day at the office.

I was staring down—or maybe I was *being* stared down —by none other than the country's (or was it the world's?) most massive teen queen pop star. Five-foot-one and ninety-ish pounds of spray-on tan, bleached pink/blonde hair, fake blue contact lenses, and a shit ton of bad attitude.

And I was rapidly on my way from being annoyed at her media whoring to flat-out hating her, *if* I were to be really honest about it. Too bad I hated her music, not that she'd ever give me a concert ticket or free MP3, anyway.

But she was my client, I was her lawyer, and I had to eat all the shit she threw my way. She paid my law firm more money in a year than some people made in a lifetime.

"Shaley, you know these accusations are serious, right?" I asked, trying to catch her attention.

But she just looked out the windows of the twenty-fourth floor of the tallest building in Los Angeles, home to the boutique entertainment law firm, Roman, Bishop, Kramer. Also known as RBK, my place of employment, where I was a junior attorney on the fast track to *great things*.

At least that's what they dangled in front of me on a regular basis to get me to work harder, as if that were even possible. As it was, I worked from seven in the morning to ten at night six days a week. On the nights I was slacking, I'd leave work at, god forbid, nine. I knew by heart the menu of every take-out restaurant in a mile radius of both my office and my home. I cooked so seldom, there was dust on my stove, and I wasn't sure whether the oven actually worked. I'd never opened it.

I forced a deep breath, usually a good move when I was about to lose it, when I realized I was gripping my pen so hard my fingers were turning white. For a brief moment, I fantasized about stabbing someone with it.

"Shaley? Shaley, are you okay?" I asked in my fake-patient voice. I'd learned a few tone-of-voice tricks, and many other *difficult client techniques*, from my mentor at the firm, Herschel Perkins. They'd served him well for thirty years and had made him millions, so who was I to buck the tried and true?

But on that particular day, Hershel's golden trade secrets weren't working all that well. So I turned to Shaley's watchdog dad, who accompanied her everywhere.

"Mr. Landers? Shaley seems kind of preoccupied…"

Or, just fucking rude, not that I could say that. People like me, who are on track for *great things*, as the firm was so fond of saying, kept thoughts like that to ourselves. Where they could rot our insides.

Shaley's dad leaned across our expensive conference room table, into which his pop star daughter was carving her initials with a pen she'd swiped from reception. Was furniture damage billable? I made a note to ask the office manager.

He turned from his daughter to me. "Miss Delaney— hey, can I call you Dove?" he asked.

*No, I'd prefer if you treated me like a professional who went to law school and not your waitress at TGI Fridays…*but my hands were tied. "Yes, of course."

Shaley's dad, Mr. Landers, wore on his fingers big gold rings that he liked to twirl, and a thick gold chain around his neck. He was a sweaty, overweight man, whom someone must have recently brought to a spa as evidenced by his perfectly waxed and trimmed eyebrows. Their shape was so unnatural, I could hardly look away.

He leaned onto the conference table, hands folded, which made the finger fat around his rings bulge. "Dove, my little Shaley here is under an enormous amount of pressure. She's just back from tour, has a month to record a new album, and then has to hit the road again right away. That's a lot for a eighteen-year-old." He sat back, smiling and satisfied with his mansplaining, as if I didn't know pretty much what she did every hour of every day.

For heaven's sake, RBK was the entertainment law firm that represented every single thing she did.

Her endorsement deal with Puma? I negotiated it.

Her TV ad for Pepsi? Did that one, too.

Hell, the executive producers of SNL and I were on a daily call basis for a while when she was trying to get the same date as the latest James Bond actor as guest host.

I practically knew when the kid went to the bathroom. Not that I wanted to—it was just part of my job, all the while hating her sticky-sweet, off-pitch, nonsensical music. That she wrote, herself. Words *and* music.

Supposedly.

And that's how we got to the meeting we were having that day.

I took a deep breath and forced a smile, which I knew would make my tone of voice go where it needed to. Another Herschel trick.

"I know, Mr. Landers." I nodded in solidarity with his obvious awe of his child, whose success clearly paid for all his gold jewelry and spa eyebrows. "I don't know how she does it. And I don't know how you manage it all. You people are just amazing."

Whew, that was some deep BS. Seriously award-winning BS.

But now they were listening. Both of them.

So I jumped all over their attention. "Given all your hard work and commitments, that makes it even worse that you're being sued for copyright infringement by The Freaks. I mean, we all know there's bad blood between you, Shaley, and their lead singer. But c'mon, how can those people go after your livelihood?"

Said bad blood was related to a leaked sex video the lead singer had released when Shaley dumped his ass. It was all over *People* magazine, and the injunctions had taken our firm weeks to file and a lot of legal wrangling on my part. But in the end, RBK had earned a million dollars.

And me? Well, I got sick from lack of sleep.

And now The Freaks were hitting back. If this was a boxing match, we were heading into the middle rounds of what could prove to be a bloody shitshow of a slug fest.

Shaley had stopped carving on our ten-thousand-dollar conference table and was finally looking at me. She even nodded slightly.

"So, to protect you—" I looked at her and then her father, who pretty much viewed his only child as a walking, talking cash machine "—I need to know everything that happened. I'm going to hire a third-party expert to assess how close your riff is to The Freaks'. And if it really *is* that close, then we'll explain how you came up with the music, and how it's pure coincidence that your riffs are similar."

She finally spoke. "I hate those fuckers, and I want you to take them *down*," she growled. She looked to her dad for support, who nodded like a bobble head instead of suggesting his teenage daughter not use the word *fuck*.

Deep breath. Smile. Channel Herschel. He never lost his shit.

"Let's take care of this first, okay, before we *take them down*." I couldn't believe I even repeated those words. I was embarrassed for myself.

"Now Shaley, just for my own notes, how did you come up with the riff? In case we end up in court, you'll have to explain where it came from to prove you didn't copy it."

Her face went blank. As I suspected it might.

She fucking copied their song. I knew it.

But I was not the judge here. No, I was just the unfortunate attorney helping a dishonest and spoiled eighteen-year-old cover her ass when the thing she needed most was actually getting it kicked. You could do that if you had enough money.

And fame. Fame helped, too.

Her gaze returned to the window, just like it always did when she wanted to be a little shit. She shrugged. "I don't know."

Her dad leaned toward her and put a hand on her shoulder. "Shaley, honey? Dove is right. We really need to know how you came up with the riff. You know, to prove you thought it up yourself."

She turned to face us both, leaning back in her chair, arms crossed. "I dreamt it," she said defiantly, looking from one of us to the other to see if we were buying her bullshit.

I know *I* wasn't.

Dad, on the other hand, looked like he was ready to proclaim her answer divine intervention. Emboldened, she doubled down. "Yeah. It came to me in a dream. Like all my songs do."

In spite of the fact that my bullshit meter was buzzing off the charts, I smiled brilliantly at her award-winning lie.

And how did I know she was lying? I'm not sure I could put it into words. It was just a spidey sense lawyers got after dealing with dozens of clients, about half of whom lied their asses off on a regular basis.

And I got to represent these lovely people.

I scribbled in my notebook and slammed it shut. "Okay. Great meeting," I said, to pull things to a close. Shaley looked thrilled. Shit, if I were an eighteen-year-old, I wouldn't want to be stuck in a law office, either.

But her dad had other plans.

He stood, leaning against the window that gave us a clear shot of the Hollywood Hills when the L.A. smog wasn't too thick. His round gut hung unappealingly over his blue jeans' waistband, where he wore a giant belt buckle with his daughter's face on it.

Eww. Serious eww.

"Yes, Mr. Landers?" I stood, too, hoping they'd follow me toward the door.

He walked around the table and draped around me as if we were buds. "I was thinking, Dove, that we might get together sometime. You could come down to the marina and we could taste some bubbly on my boat. Maybe take it out for a little spin?" He beamed like he was making me the offer of a lifetime.

"Um…well, Mr. Landers—"

"Wait right there!" he said, reaching into his pocket. "First off, call me Sly, and second, here's my business card."

I took it graciously because, of course. "Thanks, um, Sly. But I'm working super-long hours now, and have very little time for socializing—"

"Stop," he bellowed, holding his hands up. "My email's on there. I'll expect to hear from you." He reached for Shaley's hand.

This kid performed her own music (supposedly) in the world's largest concert halls, earned obscene amounts of money, made sex tapes with her male teenybopper counterpart, and yet—still held her daddy's hand.

God save me.

I looked at the card her dad had thrust into my hand. His email was *readyfreddy@gmail.com*. No shit.

I *knew* that email address. I hustled back to my office after escorting them out and woke up my PC to log into Match.com, where I'd had the world's shortest experiment with online dating. I scrolled through my not-yet-closed account, and navigated to the folder labeled 'dick pics.'

And there was readyfreddy@gmail.com, in my dick pic folder. Yup, Shaley Landers' dad sent dick pics to women on online dating sites. I clicked *open* on the attachment and was greeted by a two-inch non-erect penis with a hand nearly strangling it to make it look a little bigger, surrounded by a gigantic bush of never-been-trimmed pubic hair.

That's when I closed my Match account for good.

Most important thing I'd do all day.

∼

"Heya, kiddo."

Herschel, sticking his head in my office, loved to call me kiddo. I smiled back, wishing I could think of some kind way to ask him to stop doing that without coming across as a jerk. But I couldn't. He called everyone who wasn't a named partner in the firm *kiddo*.

And he didn't mind that I called him by an abbreviated version of his first name back. So there was that.

"Hey, Hersch. Come on in," I said, gesturing to the chair opposite my desk, as if he needed an invite into my office. The man was the firm's managing partner. He could sit wherever he damn well pleased.

"How'd it go with our little pop star?" he asked, grinning.

I sighed. "Fine, I guess. I mean, I am sure she copied the other band's riff. I just know it. So I'm going to be busting my hump trying to do every trick, spin, backflip, and maneuver I can think of to keep us from losing this. The worst of it is, I don't think Shaley—or her father—have any remorse whatsoever about the whole thing, so the idea of getting them to just settle it? Not gonna happen. And the likelihood of it happening again? Very high."

Herschel shook his head. "Well, just wait until someone copies *her* music. They'll be up in arms so fast it won't even be funny. I've seen it a dozen times. People 'borrow' from others, and it's all fine and good until it happens to them. Just hang in there, and remember how valuable a client they are to the firm."

And there it was. The bottom line.

Standing in the doorway, he paused. "I meant to ask you. Heard anything about your twin sister?"

Right. My client meeting had taken Delilah, my twin, off my mind for a few blessed moments. But now that she was back to being front and center in my thoughts, the acid in my stomach churned.

I rubbed my neck, where muscles were beginning to knot, and shook my head. "No. I think she got kicked out of the rehab halfway house she was staying in."

"I'll keep her in my thoughts."

Damn him. He was so kind and compassionate, a lump began to grow in my throat.

What I didn't tell him was that I was pretty sure she was sleeping on the streets again, and that just last week, on the night of my thirtieth birthday—no, make that on the night of *our* thirtieth birthdays—I'd left work and spent hours driving around the streets, looking for her. I'd only called it quits when the sun started coming up and I had to get home to get ready for work.

My cell phone buzzed with a text, dragging me out of my reverie.

drinks? tonight?

Cosima. My BFF since kindergarten, and the one person who could shine a light on any shitty day.

yeah. I'll cut out early.

you better!

In the end, I shouldn't have cut out early. God knew I had a ton of work to do, not least of which was a refresher on any past entertainment cases where folks had 'borrowed' others' work. But I was desperate for a break. Besides, that's what paralegals were for, and the firm had some good ones. So, when I hoped no one was looking, I got up from my desk as if I were heading to the ladies' room, and ran for the elevator. I wasn't sure why I felt so compelled to sneak. I mean, I'd be coming back to the office to do more work afterward, anyway.

I dashed into our favorite 'quick drink' bar and spotted my beautiful friend as soon as my eyes adjusted to the dim light.

"Dove!" Cosima said, leaving a big red lipstick mark on my cheek. "You look awesome, rocking that girlie look." She flipped her expensively highlighted blonde hair back over her shoulder. In her slim pencil skirt and sky-high pumps, she was the epitome of professional-girl chic, so a compliment from her was worth its weight in gold.

I looked down ay my full skirt, smoothing it out. My style was entirely different, but I hoped just as cool. "Oh my god, *so* good to see you," I said, as we settled onto barstools at the joint a few blocks from my office. There were closer bars, but I couldn't risk running into someone from work.

I ordered a glass of zinfandel, and Cosima ordered some floofy drink I couldn't even pronounce. Because she was the hip and arty one, she always knew the latest cool cocktails. Actually, she knew the latest cool everything. It'd been this way since we were kids, and she was helping me with my clothes while I helped her memorize the presidents for history class.

"Do you really have to go back to work after this?" she asked, taking a sip of her bright green concoction.

I nodded. "Yeah. I do. Got some stuff to review."

"Oh my god, that law firm treats you like a damn slave. I hope they're paying you a fuckload of money." She tapped a perfectly manicured nail on the bar to make her point. I looked down at my own sad and neglected nails that hadn't been properly groomed in a year. Or longer.

"Well, the idea is that the *fuckload of money*, as you call it, will come my way *in time*. Supposedly." I felt an immediate buzz from the wine and realized I'd not eaten since the morning. After all, when you work fourteen to sixteen hours a day behind a desk, the only way to keep any sort of figure was to not eat much. If at all.

"Oh shit, don't look now…" she said.

Which means, as everyone knows, that you *should* look.

Cripes. I shouldn't have looked. It was Rick. Also known as *Rick the Dick*. With our hoochie-mama receptionist.

Yeah, I'd made the dumb-ass rookie associate mistake of sleeping with someone at the office who, after our second booty call, started avoiding me in the office. Come to find out, he was through with me and on to the receptionist. The *receptionist*.

"Ugh. Look at her. She must suck cock like a Hoover. And those tits. How does she not tip over?" Cosima said, turning up her nose, her lips green from her drink. And somehow she still looked amazing.

I could always count on her to take my side.

"You know what you need to do, honey?" she said, setting down her now- empty glass. "Go get yourself one of those killer massages. You know, at the Avalon."

Now that was an idea. A very smart move. A person could only take so much incoming bullshit at once, and I deserved a little break. Or a big one as the case might be. And Avalon was just the ticket.

Read more of Dove's story…

ALSO BY MIKA LANE

The Anti-Hero Chronicles
Dirty Game / Audio
Nasty Bet / Audio
Filthy Deal / Audio

The Savage Mountain

Men Reverse Harem Series
The Captive / Audio
The Runaway / Audio
The Pursued / Audio
The Prize / Audio
Boxset books 1-4 / Audio

Contemporary Reverse Harem
The Inheritance / Audio
The Renovation / Audio
The Promotion / Audio
The Gallery / Audio
The Collection / Audio
Boxset books 1-5

A Player Romance series 1-3
Mister Hollywood
Mister Fake Date
Mister Wrong

Billionaire Duet 1-2
Dirty Little Secret
Sinful Little Betrayal

STAY IN THE KNOW
Join my Insider Group
Exclusive access to private release specials, giveaways, the

opportunity to receive advance reader copies (ARCs), and other random musings.

LET'S KEEP IN TOUCH
Mika Lane Newsletter
Email me
Visit me! www.mikalane.com
Friend me! Facebook
Pin me! Pinterest
Follow me! Twitter
Laugh with me! Instagram

ABOUT THE AUTHOR

Dear Reader:

Please join my Insider Group and be the first to hear about giveaways, sales, pre-orders, ARCs, and other cool stuff: http://mikalane.com/join-mailing-list.

Writing has been a passion of mine since, well, forever (my first book was "The Day I Ate the Milkyway," a true fourth-grade masterpiece). These days, steamy romance, both dark and funny, gives purpose to my days and nights as I create worlds and characters who defy the imagination. I live in magical Northern California with my own hand-some alpha dude, sometimes known as Mr. Mika Lane, and an evil cat named Bill. These two males also defy my imagination from time to time.

A lover of shiny things, I've been known to try to new recipes on unsuspecting friends, find hiding places so I can read undisturbed, and spend my last dollar on a plane ticket somewhere.

I have several titles for you to choose from including the perennially favorite Billionaire and Reverse Harem stories.

And have you see my Player Series about male escorts who make the ladies of Hollywood curl their toes and forget their names? Hottttt.... And my brand new anti-hero/mafia books are coming out in audio as I write this.

Exciting news: in June 2020, I will be publishing with Vi Keeland's and Penelope Ward's Cocky Hero Club as one of their contributing authors. Stay tuned for more on this or follow my Facebook page: https://www.facebook.com/mikalaneauthor. And, as if that's not cool enough, I am also writing in K. Bromberg's Everyday Heroes world. Look for that later in the year.

I'll always promise you a hot, sexy romp with kick-ass but imperfect heroines, and some version of a modern-day happily ever after.

I LOVE to hear from readers when I'm not dreaming up naughty tales to share. Join my Insider Group so we can get to know each other better http://mikalane.com/join-mailing-list, or contact me here: https://mikalane.com/contact.

xoxo
   Love,
   Mika